A BELOW STAIRS MYSTERY COLLECTION

BELOW STAIRS MYSTERIES

JENNIFER ASHLEY

JA / AG PUBLISHING

Cover design by Kim Killion

CONTENTS

A SOUPÇON OF POISON

INTRODUCTORY NOTE

A Soupçon of Poison begins the Kat Holloway Below Stairs Mysteries, and introduces Kat, Daniel, James, and Grace. Events take place before the first full-length novel, *Death Below Stairs.*

CHAPTER 1

LONDON, 1880

I am a cook, and better than most, even at my young age of nine and twenty, and the gentry and aristocracy pay highly to have me.

Sir Lionel Leigh-Bradbury of Portman Square gave me less than I might have had elsewhere, but when the agency told me he'd agreed to the large number of days out a month I'd requested, I leapt at the position.

I had never actually met Sir Lionel—the housekeeper and the agency made all the negotiations with me—until I'd been in his employ nearly two months. Then, one evening, he abruptly summoned me.

Copley, the thin, sour-faced butler with a walleye, delivered the news to the kitchen. "'Is royal 'ighness demands your presence. In 'is library."

I stilled my knife on the carcass of an onion spread before me. *"Now?"* I asked crossly.

I had much work to prepare for supper, having no assistant. Sir Lionel employed only one footman and a scullery maid in addition to housekeeper, butler, and cook. He kept the housekeeper and butler only because he'd inherited them with the house and title.

Copley banged down his salver and threw himself into a chair by the fire. "No," he snarled. "'E must 'ave meant in a fortnight."

Copley despised all women in general and me in particular. He was pinch-faced, bad-tempered and usually half drunk with gin.

I began chopping again, with more vigor this time. "He stays above stairs, and I stay below," I said. "It is the proper way of things."

"Am I to blame for 'is upbringing? You'd best get to it, woman."

I sighed, finished the onion, and carefully washed my knife before putting it away. Onion juice left to dry can be disastrous to cutlery. I put the onions in a bowl, wiped my hands, and went to face my employer for the first time.

Sir Lionel sat alone in the library on the second floor. The high-ceilinged, dark-beamed room was cold, musty, and dimly lit. Tall bookcases lined the room, each packed so tightly with books I doubted that any could be pried out and actually read.

My employer reposed at a writing table with about a dozen photographs on it. As I came as close as I dared, I saw that the photos were of older Leigh-Bradburys, of Sir Lionel in formal dress, and one of a young woman, pretty, whom I did not recognize. That photo looked old, but the frame was new, so perhaps it was a beloved sister or beau who had passed away.

Sir Lionel had limp brown hair that hung from a bald place on top of his head, a white face, and a long nose. His limbs were almost as thin as Copley's, and his long coat hung on his bony shoulders. He was middle-aged and had recently inherited this house, all its contents, and his baronetcy from his uncle.

I stopped a foot or so from the desk and folded my hands on my plump abdomen. "You asked to see me, sir?"

Sir Lionel looked me up and down, his prominent Adam's apple moving. "*You* are my cook?"

I inclined my head. "I am Mrs. Holloway, sir."

"*Mrs.* Holloway." He leaned forward a little as he said the name. "You are married?"

My matrimonial state was none of his business. "All cooks are called missus, sir," I said stiffly.

Sir Lionel continued to stare at me, his blue eyes so wide they protruded. The good Lord had blessed me with a comely face—so I'd been told—a mass of curling dark hair, and a figure that was curved and not angular, but I saw no reason for such amazement.

"You sent for me, sir," I prompted as Sir Lionel continued to stare at me.

"Oh. Yes. I wanted to … I wanted …" He trailed off and assumed a fretful frown. "I am feeling unwell. The dish you prepared for my supper last night is to blame."

"The cassoulet?" I said in surprise. "Of course it was not to blame. Everyone in this house partook of that dish, and no one has any ill effects. It was perfectly fine."

"It tasted off."

"Nonsense. The chicken was freshly killed and the vegetables fine and crisp. I was lucky to get them and at a fair price."

Sir Lionel tapped the arms of his chair. "I have eaten only your cassoulet since last night, and I am ill. What else could it be?"

I eyed him critically. "If you've eaten naught else, it's no wonder you're ill. I'll make you a cup of beef tea, sir, and send you up some seedcake."

He looked indignant. "I do not want—"

"Certainly you do," I interrupted. "Your humors are out of balance and need some easing. I ate a good portion of that cassoulet, and as you can see, I am fit and hale. You want a bit of grub in your belly, that is all."

Sir Lionel gave me a dazed look, as though not used to being told what to do, even if it was for his own good. "Er, yes, quite. Yes, yes, send it up, whatever you like."

I gave him a little bow and turned away, feeling his gaze on my back all the way to the door.

Downstairs, I cut up seedcake and fixed a thick broth of beef with black pepper. I set this all on a tray, which was carried upstairs by the footman, because Copley was snoring and unlikely to rouse himself the rest of the night.

My cakes seemed to have done the trick, as did my supper of thick slices of pork, hearty bread, and onion soup, for I heard no more complaints about illness and no more words against my cooking. I did not see Sir Lionel again for another three weeks.

Late one night, after the other staff had gone to bed, I sat in the kitchen at the wide wooden table, sharpening my knives.

A cook's knives are her greatest asset, and if they go dull, they are no use at all and should be replaced. As decent knives are hideously expensive, I kept mine in good repair.

I did not trust anyone with the task of sharpening but myself, so I sat on my stool, alone, and drew a blade across the damped stone. The only sound in the silent room was the scrape of stone on steel and the hiss of the oil lamp beside me.

The solitude comforted me. I'd had a trying day. Copley's bunions had played him up, making him more sour than usual, and he'd gone so far as to throw a bowl of porridge at me. John the footman had dropped and shattered a crock full of sugar. The scullery maid had taken sick, so I'd had to do all the washing up myself.

Because of that, by the time I'd gotten to the market, all the best produce was gone. My bread had over-risen and deflated upon itself while I was out because John had been too stupid to follow the simplest instructions.

I'd made my disapprobation known, and the others had retired somewhat earlier than usual, leaving me alone with my knives.

Where Sir Lionel found me.

"Mrs. Holloway?"

I peered through the kitchen's gloom, my comfort evaporating. The master of the house stood at the door to the stairway, his breathing loud and hoarse. He moved across the flagstones to the table where I sat, and gazed at me with eyes that were sunken and petulant.

I jumped to my feet, annoyed. The kitchen was my demesne. The master might own the house, but a good employer understood that not interfering in the kitchen made for a tranquil domestic situation. Sir Lionel had his rooms above stairs where I did not trespass, and he had no reason to trespass on *me.*

"Might I help you with something, sir?" I asked, striving to remain polite.

"Good heavens, Mrs. Holloway." Sir Lionel, his voice breathy, looked past me at the table. "What is it you're doing?"

Dancing naked upon Hampstead Heath. "Just giving my knives a bit of attention, sir. I like them nice and sharp."

"Yes, I am certain you do."

Before I could decipher this comment, Sir Lionel had moved abruptly to my side and pinned me against the table. He was stronger than his size let on, and he held me fast with his spindly arms.

"Mrs. Holloway, I can think of nothing but you. Of your eyes, your hair …" He pulled a lock free from my cap. "Your bosom, so comely. Do you have children?"

"One," I gasped, the truth I kept hidden bursting out in my amazement.

He did not seem to hear me. "My nursery maid had a bosom as large as yours. She let me feast upon her."

I scarcely wanted to think about *that.* I desperately craned my head away from his port-laden breath and bloodshot eyes.

"Let me feast upon you, Katharine."

Oh, this would never do. I groped behind me across the smooth boards of the table and closed my fingers around the handle of a knife.

It was my carver. I pulled it around and brought it up right under Sir Lionel's chin.

Sir Lionel squeaked in alarm. His gaze shot to the knife then back to me, spots of red burning on his cheeks. He must have seen something in my blue eyes he so admired, because he released me and took a hasty step backward.

"Sir," I said in a hard voice. "You employ me and pay my wages. I cook. That line should *never* be crossed."

Sir Lionel's mouth opened and closed a few times. "It should not?"

"No, sir. It should not."

His petulant look returned. "But you are so beautiful."

I held the knife point steady, though I was shaking all the way through. "You flatter me, sir. I am a cook, is all. You go along upstairs and to bed. You will feel better in the morning."

"No, no …er. I am going out."

"Right, then, sir. Off you go."

Sir Lionel eyed the glinting knife blade, stared at my bosom with stark regret, turned on his heel, and marched out of the room.

Not until I'd heard him tramp all the way up the stairs and slam the door above did I let out an explosive breath and drop to the stool, the strength gone out of me.

"Fool," came a voice.

I smothered a yelp as Copley materialized from the shadows. My knife clattered to the table. "What the devil do you mean, skulking about like that?" I cried.

Copley gave me a sickly grin, his walleye gleaming. "Ye could 'ave gained some favors with 'im, woman. You give 'im a bit, and 'e gives you a rise in wages. Any sensible woman would think it a bit of luck."

"I *am* a sensible woman," I said firmly. "Which is why I told him to be gone."

"Maybe 'e'd even marry you." Copley sniggered, a dry sound.

"Oh, most like. The gentry don't marry cooks." Thank heavens. On the other hand, I might have just lost myself my post.

Copley scooted close enough to me that I could smell the gin on his breath. "I'll keep this atween you and me. Can't let it get about that you cast your eyes upon the master, can it?"

He'd turn it about and spread that story, simply because he could. "You are a little swine," I said. "I did nothing of the sort."

"But none know it but me, you, and 'is nibs, do they? And I seed 'ow quick you was to shove a knife at 'is throat."

"I only meant to frighten him." I let my tone grow chilly. "I thought it most effective. Didn't you?"

Copley's gaze slid to the knife that rested near my hand, and he faded back from me. "I'll remember it. I will." And thankfully, he shuffled away, heading upstairs to his bed.

I went back to sharpening the blades that had done me so much good tonight, but it was a long time before I could stop shaking. Longer still before I could make myself retire to my tiny bedchamber tucked behind the kitchen and sleep.

———

THE NEXT DAY, DANIEL MCADAM CAME WHISTLING DOWN THE kitchen steps to deliver a bushel of apples.

Daniel McAdam had, as we ladies put it, a way with him. I'd known him for about a year, ever since the day he'd stepped into old Mrs. Pauling's kitchens, where'd I'd formerly worked, to get out of the rain. Daniel ever after paused to flirt with me, harmless like, whenever he made a delivery to Mrs. Pauling's house, and now to Sir Lionel's.

I knew little about Daniel, even after a year. He was a man of all work and a jack of all trades. He delivered goods, carried messages, and ran far and wide about London—once I'd seen him driving a hired carriage, competently maneuvering it through the crowds.

I did not know where he lodged or where he disappeared to for weeks at a time. He'd only wink and answer evasively whenever I brought up these subjects.

I knew Daniel wasn't married because I'd asked him that, point blank. When a man flirts with a woman, she ought to know where things stand.

Daniel had dark hair and dark blue eyes and a tall, attractive body. He could read and write and was quite clever, though he never admitted to any schooling.

I concluded that he must be the son of a middle-class gentleman, possibly illegitimate, but he never spoke of his family. He turned his hand to a good many menial tasks, things even a destitute gentleman might shun, which was why I thought him a bastard son. Father genteel, mother a tavern maid or something of the sort, and now Daniel had to grub for a living.

No matter who he was, Daniel seemed to be happy puttering about London, making friends with everyone he met and doing any odd job he could.

It was a daft way to live, and I told him so. He only laughed and said: *Some of us were born to work and others to keep the devil amused.*

He always said something nonsensical when he did not want to give an answer.

This morning, Daniel set down the apples and waited with good humor while I wiped my hands of puff pastry dough and poured him a cup of steaming tea.

Daniel swallowed a long drink and grinned at Copley, who leaned against the wall, barely able to stand. "You'll kill yourself with gin, Copley." Daniel took a flask from his pocket and dropped a dollop of whiskey into his own cup.

Copley gave him a sour look. He'd woken with a raging headache and had been sick in the basin twice already. "I were up late. Woke by the master and Mrs. Holloway a'carrying on, weren't I?"

Daniel raised dark brows. I dumped a large ball of butter onto my dough and vigorously attacked the mess with my rolling pin.

"Why don't you tell 'im, Mrs. H?" Copley rasped. "About 'ow the master tried it on with you, and ye almost slit 'is throat?"

CHAPTER 2

Daniel did not change expression, but his blue gaze focused on me. "What happened, Kat?" he asked, his tone gentle.

Daniel was the only person I allowed to call me *Kat.* Not that I'd given him permission. He'd simply taken it up, and I'd not prevented him.

I rolled the pastry dough flat and used my scraper to fold each third in on itself before going at it again. Puff pastry was difficult to get right, and a kitchen full of curious people was not assisting me to concentrate.

"Nothing as interesting as Copley makes out," I said crisply.

"Even so, tell me."

When Daniel McAdam spoke in that voice—quiet and friendly, yet full of steel, people tended to obey him. I stopped pounding at the dough, which needed to rest and cool anyway, and gave him an abbreviated account of the incident. Copley snorted a few times and inserted foolish comments at intervals.

Daniel helped himself to another cup of tea, minus the whiskey this time, and sipped it as I talked. When I finished, Daniel rose from the stool where he'd been sitting and set the cup on the draining board by the sink. "Copley," he said in that steely voice. "A word, if you please."

Copley looked surprised, but as I said, people tended to obey Daniel without quite knowing why.

Copley followed Daniel across the kitchen and out the scullery door. The scullery maid, sniffling with her cold, let dirty water drip all over the flagstone floor while she watched Daniel with lovesick eyes.

I have no idea to this day what Daniel said to Copley, but when Copley returned he was subdued. He skulked across the kitchen without looking at me and stomped up the stairs.

THE VERY NEXT MORNING SIR LIONEL STARTED TAKING HIS vengeance on me for not only rejecting his advances but putting my knife to his throat. He did nothing so direct as sack me—oh, no. He went about it by more subtler means, trying to vanquish me, if you like.

Now, you may wonder why I did not simply pack up my knives and march out, but while good cooks are in demand, good places aren't all that thick on the ground. As horrible as Sir Lionel was, he lived in London, where I needed to stay, the wage was decent, and I had my many days out a month, which was the most important thing to me. So I stayed and put up with him.

Sir Lionel did not come to the kitchen again—he'd learned that lesson. He sent his demands through Mrs. Watkins, the housekeeper. Sometimes Copley delivered the messages, but even Sir Lionel realized that Copley couldn't be trusted when he was befuddled with drink, so Mrs. Watkins brought down most of his orders.

Mrs. Watkins had worked in this house for many years, previously for Sir Lionel's uncle, and she didn't think much of the current master. She was straight-backed and pinch-nosed and set in her ways, and didn't hold with all this cooking nonsense—a bit of boiled mutton was all a body needed, and any simpleton could buy that in a shop. For all her decided opinions, Mrs. Watkins wasn't a bad sort, although she didn't approve of cooks being as young as I was.

I couldn't help my age—I'd been assistant to one of the best cooks in London at fifteen, and had proved to have a talent for the job. That cook had passed on when I'd been twenty, word had spread that her apprentice could replicate her meals, and agencies fought to have me on their books.

However, I had to be choosy where I worked, and my situation with Sir Lionel, unfortunately, was ideal. Except for Sir Lionel, of course. Mrs. Watkins made it plain that Sir Lionel was a disappointment after his uncle, who'd been a true gentleman, she said, but Mrs. Watkins, like me, needed the position.

Sir Lionel began his game of revenge by sending down odd and impossible requests for his dinners—wild birds that wouldn't be in season for another few months, tender vegetables that had gone out of season months before, and dishes even I had never heard of. I had to read through my treasured tomes to find recipes for what he wanted, and some I simply had to invent. Even the exhaustive Mrs. Beeton failed me from time to time.

Some days I'd nearly make myself ill getting the meal finished to his order—I had my pride, after all—and he'd send word at the last minute that he would dine at his club and wouldn't be back until morning.

The delicate meal wouldn't keep for a day, so I and the household staff ate it. I had to watch John the footman bolt my coq a vin like it was mutton stew and listen to Mrs. Watkins complain that food should be simple without all this fuss. Copley would eat steadily, then follow the meal with a mug of gin and belch loudly.

The morning after, Sir Lionel would send down a sternly worded note that I'd spent far too much money on foodstuffs and threaten to take it out of my wages.

A lesser cook would have fled. But it built up my pride that I was mostly able to fulfill his bizarre requests and build a meal around them, no matter how much Sir Lionel made clear he did not appreciate it. I rose to the challenge, wanting to prove he could not best me.

Where he came up with his ideas for what he wanted me to cook I had no idea. Sir Lionel did not strike me as a refined gentleman with cultivated tastes. Likely he found descriptions of dishes in books, or he had a friend who made up the meals for him, laughing about the good trick they were playing on a cook who needed to learn her place.

Then came the day I nearly threw down my apron and ran out the door to never come back. Mrs. Watkins, at seven o'clock in the evening, brought me down a note telling me he wanted truffles a l'Italienne with beef in pepper sauce that night.

"Truffles?" I bellowed. "Where does he think I will find a handful of black truffles at this time of day?"

"I couldn't say." It was obvious Mrs. Watkins had no idea what a truffle was. "But he is adamant."

It was impossible. I knew all the good markets and who might have decent exotic fungi, but I had no time to get to them before they shut up for the night.

As luck would have it, an urchin I'd seen helping Daniel unload his goods a time or two was hanging around the scullery door. He'd been hoping for scraps or a chat with the scullery maid, but I stormed out to him, seized him by the ear, and told him to find Daniel for me.

"Scour the town if you must," I said. "Tell him Mrs. Holloway desperately needs his help. There's tuppence in it for you if you hurry."

The urchin jerked himself from me and rubbed his ear, but he didn't look angry. "Don't worry, missus. I'll find 'im."

The lad was true to his word. Daniel came knocking within

the hour, and the lad happily jingled the coins I dropped into his hand.

Daniel listened to me rant, his warm smile nearly enough to calm my troubles. Nearly. When I finished, Daniel held out his hand.

"Give me your list, and I'll find the things for you," he said.

"How can you?" My voice rose, tinged with hysteria. "In half an hour?"

Daniel only regarded me calmly as he took the paper upon which I'd written ingredients. "The sooner I am gone, the sooner I can return."

I let out my breath, my heart in my words. "Thank you. I don't know who you are, Daniel McAdam, but you are a godsend."

Something flickered in his dark blue eyes, but his crooked smile returned. "I've been called much worse, Kat, believe me. Back in a tick."

He did return very quickly with a bundle of all I needed, including the finest truffles I'd ever seen and a small bottle of champagne, which Sir Lionel never stocked in his cellar. I did not like to ask how Daniel had come by the rarer things, and he did not volunteer the information.

Daniel tried to refuse money for the foodstuffs. He held his up his hands, spreading his fingers wide. "It was a challenge, Kat. I never knew the intricacies of food purchasing or how many markets we have in London. Keep your money for the next meal he demands."

"Don't talk nonsense. I'll not take them as gifts. Stand there while I get you some coin."

I hurried down to the housekeeper's parlor where we kept a locked tin of cash on hand for extra expenses. Only I and Mrs. Watkins had the key to it—Copley couldn't be trusted not to spend the money on drink.

Daniel hadn't given me a tally, but I counted out what I

thought would be the cost of the goods and rushed back out, to find Daniel nowhere in sight.

"Where is Mr. McAdam?" I asked the urchin, who'd remained to make sheep's eyes at the scullery maid.

"'E's off," the urchin answered. "Said 'e couldn't wait."

"Blast the man," I said fervently.

I put the money back into the tin but vowed I'd force it upon him somehow one day. A woman couldn't afford to have a man do her expensive favors, especially a man as beguiling as Daniel McAdam. I'd learned all about the dangers of pretty men at a very young age, and I'd had enough of *that.*

Sir Lionel's next unreasonable dinner demand came the very next day. He decided, at five o'clock, if you please, that he'd entertain friends at his dinner table at seven. Mrs. Watkins brought down the order and stepped back as I read it.

Leek and cream soup, whitefish in a velouté sauce, green salad, squab stuffed with peppercorns, beef in a wine sauce, asparagus with egg, fricassee of wild mushrooms, soft rolls, a chocolate soup and a berry tart for pudding.

"Has he gone mad?" I screeched. "I haven't a scrap of chocolate in the house, no hope of fresh fish or game birds today." I flung the paper to the table. "That is the last straw, Mrs. Watkins. Either we come to an understanding or I give my notice. I ought to simply give it now and leave, let him and his guests do with salt pork and potatoes."

Copley, lounging in his chair near the fire, cackled. "Mrs. H. can't do it. All I hear is what a grand cook she is, how everyone wants her, how she's wasted in this 'ouse. She's asked to cook a few bits of fish, and she 'as hysterics. If you're so sought after, my girl, why ain't ye cooking for dukes, or for one of the royals?"

I dragged in a breath, trying to ignore Copley. "I agree that if I can pull this meal together it would make my reputation. But . . . oh—"

"Would it?" Mrs. Watkins picked up the list again, which she'd written in her careful hand at Sir Lionel's dictation. "I confess, I've never heard of velouté or eaten chocolate soup."

"Well, you shall eat it tonight. You, Mr. Copley, can cease laughing at me and help. I shall need a good bottle of sweet white wine and a robust red for the beef sauce and the chocolate. A claret for the table. *Asparagus*—I ask you. Any I can find will be woody and tasteless. But perhaps . . ." I trailed off, my inventive mind taking over.

"Ye can't be wanting *three* bottles," Copley said, sitting up. "The master comes over snarling if I open more than one a day."

"If he wants this food and wants it done well, he'll not quibble."

Copley scowled, unhappy, but he stomped away to fetch what I needed. I always thought it a mercy Copley found wine sour and without a good kick or Sir Lionel's wine collection, a fine one built up by his uncle, would be long gone.

"How many at table?" I asked Mrs. Watkins.

"Three," she said, folding her hands. Her long string of keys hung from her belt like a jailer's. "The master and two guests, a Mr. and Mrs. Fuller."

"At least he didn't invite twenty," I said. "Small blessings, I suppose." I scanned the kitchen, and sure enough, found Daniel's lad and the scullery maid outside together on the steps.

"You," I called to the youth from the back door—I really ought to learn his name. "If you find Mr. McAdam for me in half an hour, this time I'll give you a shilling."

The boy grinned, saluted me, and off he went.

CHAPTER 3

Daniel came in twenty minutes. I explained my predicament, and again, he showed no qualms about searching the city for all I needed.

"How can you?" I asked, handing him the list I'd written out. "I *could* find all this, if I had a day or two."

Daniel shrugged. His dark hair was spotted with rain, which had begun to fall hard. Perhaps we'd have a flood, and Sir Lionel's guests wouldn't be able to come.

"My deliveries take me all over London," Daniel said. "I know who has what, who can get what."

He spoke easily, as though producing expensive foodstuffs out of the air was nothing. "What on earth do you deliver?" I asked.

Another shrug. "This and that." Daniel winked, actually tweaked my nose, and then disappeared up the stairs, whistling.

"That man is trouble," Mrs. Watkins said darkly, folding her arms as she watched him go.

"Daniel? I mean, Mr. McAdam?" I quickly turned to start scrubbing down my work table. "He's a kind soul, is all."

"Hmph." Mrs. Watkins made a motion of dusting off her

hands. "I say trouble. Well, I must get on making sure the house is to rights. Sally!" she shouted at the scullery maid. "Get in here and wash up those dishes, girl, or I'll take a strap to you."

———

DANIEL RETURNED MORE QUICKLY THAN I'D THOUGHT HE COULD. I was in the butler's pantry, arguing with Copley about the wine, when Daniel arrived, dumped several boxes next to my work table, and disappeared again.

Copley did know a surprising amount about wine, which explained why he kept his post as butler, plus he could put on a toffy accent for the guests when he chose. I finally came away with a decent German Riesling and a deep red Côtes du Rhône, with his promise to decant the best of the claret.

By the time I emerged, Daniel had come and gone. I was disappointed not to speak to him, but I was soon too busy to think more about it.

Daniel had brought me everything I needed, even fresh fish. They were perfectly fine, firm, slick, with no fishy smell to clog up the kitchen.

Now to prepare all these dishes in no time at all, including a white sauce that needed to simmer, and make feather-light rolls to go with everything.

If I'd been in a larger household, with several assistants, I could do this meal in a trice. As it was, I was soon in despair. The fish had to be cleaned, the fowls plucked and readied, the vegetables scrubbed and chopped. The velouté had to be constantly stirred so the delicate thickened stock didn't burn, the tart shells formed, chilled, and baked. I gave vent to my feelings, which only sent everyone else running away, leaving me on my own.

Almost. As I was up to my arms in fish entrails, the urchin came tripping into the kitchen without so much as a by-your-leave.

"I don't have any more errands for you," I said to him in irritation.

The lad, not cowed, didn't leave. "Mr. McAdam sent me. He says whatever you need help with, I was to do, even if it were cooking."

I stared at him in surprise. He was a sturdy young man, about fifteen, I'd say, with strong-looking hands. He was also filthy.

"John!" I bellowed. The footman popped his head around the corner from the servants' hall, where he was frantically polishing silver. I pointed my bloody fillet knife at the urchin. "Get him cleaned up and lend him some clothes. You can't come near this kitchen, lad, until all that dirt is off you. No one wants fleas in their dinner. Make sure he scrubs his hair, John. With soap."

John nodded solemnly, the urchin sent me a grin, and both youths were off.

When the urchin returned, he was urchin no longer. Now that his hair was clean, I saw it gleam dark red. His face was freckled, a fact I hadn't been able to detect under the grime, and his eyes were clear and brown. He had even teeth and good breath, and he'd trimmed his nails and scrubbed under them. John had lent him some trousers, shirt, and coat, all of which were a bit tight, but he'd do.

"What's your name?" I asked him.

The lad shrugged, an imitation of Daniel's. "You can call me James."

Which meant that might or might not be his name, but I had no time to quibble. "Very well, James, I need you to prepare this fowl for me. Here's how you do it . . ."

James proved quite competent. I could tell he'd never done any cookery before, but he was a quick learner, and worked steadily, without idle chatter or asking useless questions. Between the two of us, I prepared a meal a duchess would swoon over.

Perhaps I *would* seek out a duchess, one who stayed in town much of the time, and show her what fine dishes I could contrive.

But the main reason I did not seek out a society hostess was because working in smaller houses for bachelors like Sir Lionel meant I had much time to myself. Not today, obviously, but most of the time. A cook working for a duchess who had dinner parties every day would be laboring from dawn to midnight, never mind how many underlings she had. I had reason to want to come and go as often as I could, and so I stayed in houses like this one.

The finished meal did me proud. I thanked James profusely, asked him to sup with the rest of us, and happily gave him a few more shillings. The dishes went up to the dining room via the lift in the corner, and Mrs. Watkins saw that all was served.

Why not Copley? Because he'd fled the house while I had been ordering everyone about in the kitchen, got roaring drunk, and collapsed when he finally came back in. John and James carried him off to bed, which left Mrs. Watkins and John to see to the dining room. Mrs. Watkins was angry at this turn of events, but I knew she'd manage.

Every plate came back scraped clean. My pride puffed up. They'd loved it.

I was, as far as I was concerned that night, the greatest cook in the land.

IT WAS LATE BEFORE I CRAWLED OFF, EXHAUSTED, TO SEEK MY BED. My bedroom was a cubby-hole of a chamber, but I liked it because it lay right behind the kitchen fireplace, which kept it warm and dry.

I was deep in the slumber of the just when the scullery maid, Sally, shook me awake into darkness. "Oh, Mrs. Holloway," she said breathlessly. "There's someone above stairs."

I screwed my eyes shut against the flickering flame of her candle. "Of course there's someone above stairs. Likely his royal highness stumbling to bed after drinking himself into a stupor."

"No, ma'am. It ain't Sir Lionel." Sally regarded me in terror. "The guests left hours ago, and the master dragged 'imself off to bed already. It ain't John or Copley neither. I 'eard 'em snoring when I passed their rooms. And Mrs. Watkins went off to visit her sister."

I levered myself to a sitting position. I did not ask why Sally hadn't woken the men instead of trotting all the way downstairs to me. Copley and John would be useless and we both knew it.

"Get the poker then, girl. If it's burglars, we'll set about them."

Sally's eyes grew even more round. I threw back the covers and swung my feet to the floor, pressing them into my slippers. Sally scuttled into the kitchen and wrested the poker from its place with so much clanking I was sure the thieves would hear and run away directly.

I didn't bother with my knives. They were suited to hacking chickens, chopping onions, and frightening overly amorous masters. For fending off marauders, a poker or a stout stick works much better. To use a knife, you must get close, and those you're fighting might have something just as nasty to hand.

I took the poker from Sally, bade her bring her candle, gathered my dressing gown about me, and led the way up into the darkened house.

Sir Lionel's house, on the north side of Portman Square, was typical of those in London at the time. We climbed the back stairs to the ground floor, emerging into a hall that ran the length of the house. A staircase with polished banisters and carved newel posts rose along one side of the hall, leading to the floors above us. Rooms opened from the opposite wall of this staircase—reception room and formal dining room on the ground floor, drawing rooms on the next floor, private chambers, including the library, above that.

I went into the dining room after checking that the front door was still bolted. The walls in there were dark wood panels hung with paintings I suspected were not very good. No expensive artwork for Sir Lionel.

The room was empty. The dining table had been cleared, a cloth cover draped over it to keep it clean between meals. The chairs were straight, the curtains drawn. Nothing to be seen.

The reception room was likewise empty, nothing disturbed, no open windows anywhere.

I was beginning to believe Sally had dreamed it all, but one never knew. A thief could have forced open a back window and be merrily burgling the house above us.

I led Sally on up the stairs. We checked the front and rear drawing rooms and found nothing amiss.

I'd check one more floor and then retire to bed. If Sir Lionel wasn't stirring, then Sally had heard John or Copley moving about for whatever their reasons.

On the next floor, I saw that the door to Sir Lionel's library stood ajar. It was dark inside the room, no glow of a fire, lamp, or candle.

While I did not truly believe thieves would grope around in absolute darkness for valuables in Sir Lionel's library, the open door made me uneasy. I heard no sound within, not a rustle or thump of books as burglars searched for hidden caches of jewels.

I noiselessly pushed the door open and went inside.

Whatever fire had burned that day in the grate had smoldered to ashes. Sally kept bumping into the back of me, because she held the candle and stared into the flame until she was night-blind. But I could see a bit by the streetlight that glittered through the front windows, the curtains wide open.

What I saw was Sir Lionel. He was slumped forward over his desk, his head turned to the side, his mouth open, eyes staring sightlessly. My carving knife was buried to the hilt in his back.

Sally screeched and dropped the candle. I snatched the candle from the floor before a spark could catch the rug on fire, and raised the light high.

My entire body went numb, no feeling anywhere. “May God have mercy,” I croaked, my throat tight and dry. “What a waste of a carver. And them so dear.”

CHAPTER 4

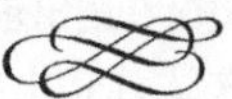

I woke John in his attic chamber—Copley heard Sally's scream and came down on his own. I sent John for the constable but ordered Copley to stay with the body while I went downstairs and dressed myself.

By time I returned to the library, the constable, a lad I'd seen walking his beat on the square, had arrived with an older sergeant. They'd lit up the room with every lamp and candle they could find and stoked the fire high. I imagined Sir Lionel's ghost cringing at the expense.

The sergeant, a squat, fat man with one string of hair across his bald pate and a wide, thick-lipped mouth, turned to me.

"It's *your* knife, eh?"

Copley looked innocently at the ceiling, but I knew he must have been filling the constable's ears with tales of my adventures with Sir Lionel.

"Of course it is mine," I snapped. "It came from the kitchens."

"'E made a grab for ye tonight, did 'e?" the sergeant asked. "And so you stuck your knife into 'im?"

I stared in astonishment. "Of course not. I've been in bed asleep these past hours. Why would I have come to the library in the middle of the night, in any case? My bedchamber is next to the kitchen, and I have no need to be above stairs at all."

The sergeant did not look impressed. "'E made a grab for you afore this, didn't 'e? And you stuck your knife to 'is throat?"

I switched my glare to Copley. He wouldn't meet my eye, but a smile hovered around his thin mouth. I said tartly, "That was weeks ago, and it was only to frighten him. I certainly would *not* have plunged my knife into a side of beef like Sir Lionel Leigh-Bradbury. It would ruin the knife. Carvers are expensive."

The constable's eyes glittered a way I didn't like. "But it was *your* knife. It would be 'andy."

"Absolute nonsense. Why would I carry my kitchen knife upstairs to the master's rooms?"

"Because 'e sent for you, and you were frightened. You brought your knife to make you feel safe-like."

"Don't be ridiculous. If I'd feared to answer his summons, I'd have stayed securely in my kitchen, or asked John to come with me. He's quite a strong lad."

The sergeant pointed a broad finger at me. "You 'ad a go at 'im before, Mr. Copley says. This time, you went too far, and did 'im."

My mouth went dry, but I kept up my bravado. "I did not kill him, you ignorant lout. Why should I?"

"Who did then? With your sticker?"

I clenched my hands. "Anyone could have taken the knife from the kitchen."

"Mr. Copley says you keep 'em put away special. No one else would know where."

"Copley does," I pointed out.

Copley sneered at me. "Bitch. She stabbed 'im. She must 'ave."

I put my closed fists on my hips. "Who says so? Did you see me, Mr. Copley?"

"Yes."

My mouth popped open. He was a liar, but Copley's look was so certain that the sergeant believed him.

"I 'eard a noise and came down," Copley said. "And there was you, a-bending over the master's body, holding the knife."

Bloody man. "Of course I looked him over when I found him here," I said, trying not to sound desperate. "He was already dead. And *you* saw nothing at all, Mr. Copley. You only came charging in because Sally was screaming, *after* we found him."

Copley scowled. "I saw ye, I tell ye."

"You saw me discovering the knife, not plunging it in," I countered, but my blood was cold. "Ask Sally." But when I looked about for the scullery maid, I did not see her or hear her anywhere.

The sergeant was obviously on Copley's side, the young constable and John confused. All men against one woman.

"No more o' this," the sergeant said severely. "You'll promenade down to the magistrate with me, missus, and he can hear your story."

My body went colder still. If I could not convince the magistrate of my innocence, I would be thrown to the wolves—or at least, to an Old Bailey trial and a jury. A long bench of men would gaze at me disapprovingly and pronounce that cooks should not stick their carving knives into their masters. And that would be the end of me.

At twenty-nine summers, I found life sweet, and I had more to live for than just myself.

I wanted to bolt. To run, run, run, snatch up my daughter from where I'd hidden her and flee. To the countryside—no, not far enough. The Continent, or farther, to Asia, perhaps, where I could cook for some colonial nabob who wouldn't care too much what I ran from as long as I could give him his familiar English fare.

I closed my eyes, and I prayed. I hadn't gone to church in about half a dozen years, but praying and church are two different things. I begged God to have mercy on me, and I opened my eyes again.

"Very well, then," I said, straightening my shoulders. "But no cuffs, if you please. I am a respectable woman."

I lifted my chin and marched before them out of the room, down the stairs, and straight out of the house.

THE MAGISTRATE WHO EXAMINED ME AT BOW STREET WAS A JOVIAL man whose rotund body betrayed that he liked his meals and missed few. I had to stand up before him while those also awaiting examination filled the room behind me—I was a nobody, and warranted no special treatment.

Most of the people at the house had been arrested in the night for theft, drunkenness, fighting, being loud and disorderly, and for prostitution. A few well-dressed solicitors wandered the crowd, looking for clients to take to barristers, but they didn't bother approaching me. I had a bit of money put by, but I doubted I'd be able to afford an eloquent, wigged barrister to argue in my defense.

The magistrate's chair creaked as he leaned over his bench and peered at me nearsightedly. "Name?"

"Katharine Holloway, sir," I said, though it was sure to be on the paper his clerk had handed him.

"And you were the mistress of Sir Lionel Leigh-Bradbury of Portman Square?"

I gave him a look of shock. "Indeed not, sir. I was his cook."

The magistrate stared at me with unblinking, light blue eyes. "His cook? Well, madam ... you certainly cooked his goose."

The stuffy room rang with laughter.

"I did not murder him, sir," I declared over the noise.

"You claim to be innocent of this crime, do you?" the magistrate asked. "Even though the butler saw you chopping his onions?" More laughter.

"Mr. Copley saw nothing," I said indignantly. "He is a drunken fool and a liar. Besides, it was a carving knife, not a chopper."

The magistrate lost his smile. "It makes no difference whether it were for skewering or filleting. The butler saw you with your sticker, and he stands by that. Do you have any witnesses as to your character? Someone who might argue for you?"

I thought quickly. Daniel leapt to mind, but I had no way of knowing where to find him. Besides, why should he speak for me, when we were only friends in passing? This magistrate, with his obnoxious sense of humor, might accuse me of being Daniel's mistress as well.

"No, sir," I said stiffly. "My family is gone. I am on my own."

"You sound proud of that fact. No woman should be pleased she has no one to take care of her."

I raised my chin. "I take care of myself."

The magistrate studied me over his bench, and I read the assessment in his face: *No better than she ought to be.*

"You take care of yourself by giving your master supper and then stabbing him through the heart?" the magistrate demanded. "I suppose you thought him ... *well served.*"

His clerks and constables as well as many of London's unwashed, roared again. I suppose this magistrate spent all his quiet time inventing quips to bring out when the opportunity arose, for the entertainment of the court.

The magistrate gave me a wide smile, betraying that his back teeth were going rotten. "Katherine Holloway, I am binding you over for the willful murder of Sir Lionel Leigh-Bradbury of Portman Square. You will be taken to Newgate to await your trial. That will give you time to *simmer in your own sauce.*"

The room went positively riotous.

I was icy with fear but refused to bow my head. I stood there, staring at the magistrate until he signaled to his bailiff. The bailiff, a tall man with wiry hair, seized my arm and pulled me from the room.

The jailer who led me to a cell in Newgate had legs far longer than mine, and I had to scuttle swiftly to keep up with him.

He took me down a flight of stairs to a chilly room already filled with people. The jailer shoved me roughly inside then retreated and locked the door. I stumbled and collided with a stone wall, pins falling from my hair, the dark mass of it tumbling down. I clung to that wall, unwilling to turn and face the crowd behind me.

What on earth was I to do? Who could help me? I needed a solicitor, but as I said, I doubted I could secure even the cheapest brief to stand up for me. I might appeal to Daniel, because he'd been kind to me, but even if he would be willing to help, I had no idea how to find him or where to send him word.

Daniel might not be in London at all. He disappeared from the metropolis now and again for weeks at a time, I supposed to work other odd jobs. I could send someone to search for him or for James, but still I had no way of knowing where to start looking—except at posh houses where he *might* make deliveries—nor anyone to send.

I turned around and slid down the wall to sit with my knees against my chest. I could not remain here. It was not only my own well-being I thought of—I took care of my daughter with my wages, and what would become of her if no more money went to the family she lived with? They were kind people, but not wealthy enough to care for a child not their own. No, I had to get out.

But perhaps Daniel would hear of my arrest. He'd go to Portman Square on his usual rounds and find me gone. The newspapers, not to mention the neighbors' servants, would be full of the tale of Sir Lionel's murder.

Then again, Daniel might believe with everyone else that I'd killed Sir Lionel. He'd go about his business, thinking himself well rid of me. I'd be convicted by a jury and hanged, my feet twisting in the breeze. Copley would come to the hanging and laugh at me.

Anger at Copley nudged away despair. If I survived this, so

help me, I would exact my revenge on the man. I had only a vague idea how I'd go about doing so, but I would have plenty of time to think.

The window high in the wall darkened, and I grew hungry. My fellow inmates slumped around me, grumbling quietly among themselves. The stink of urine, sweat, and human confinement blanketed the room.

"Eat this, luv. You'll feel better."

I looked up. The woman who stood over me had snarled red hair and smelled of gin and sweat, but the look in her blue eyes was kindly. Her red satin dress was almost clean and well-mended, as though she kept it carefully, but it hung on her thin frame without stays.

Her costume made me guess her profession. Yesterday, I would have swept by such a woman, perhaps thinking on the evils of the world that drove women to lowly things—where I might be myself had I not been lucky enough to learn cookery. Today, as the woman smiled at me and held out a bit of pasty, I wanted to embrace her as a sister.

She placed the cold pie into my hands and sat down next to me as I took a hungry bite. The pie was soggy and laden with salt, nothing like the light-crusted savory concoctions I baked myself. But at the moment, it tasted like the finest cake.

"Me name's Anne," the woman said. "You're wrong about me, you know, luv. I'm an actress."

I studied her with renewed interest but could not remember seeing her on a stage at Drury Lane or Haymarket. However, the fact that she was an actress did not necessarily mean she was a principal—one could be buried in the chorus, quietly anonymous.

"I was unjustly accused," I said, brushing a tear from my cheek.

"Ain't we all, luv? But me old lad will come for me."

Alas, I did not have an old lad, but I did have a lass who needed to be taken care of. If perhaps I *did* get word to Daniel, I would at least ask him to see that she got the stash of money I had managed to put by. Daniel could be trusted with that, I felt certain.

But now that I had time to think, what did I know about Daniel, really? Next to nothing. He'd been a bolstering help to me these last few weeks, and he flirted with me, but in a friendly, harmless way. He never tried anything improper, though he must know by now that I might not say no to improper advances from Daniel McAdam.

I knew nothing of Daniel beyond that. Not where he dwelled or who his family was nor what he did when I did not see him. I only knew that I wanted to lean my head against his strong shoulder, feel him stoke my hair, and hear him say, "There now, Kat. Never you worry. I'll see to everything."

I chewed on the pasty and remained miserable.

THE NEXT MORNING, ANNE WAS RELEASED. I CLUNG TO HER HAND when she said good-bye, knowing hers might be the last kind face I ever saw. I begged her to look for a man called Daniel McAdam and tell him what had become of me. She promised to do her best.

Anne went out, and I cried. I wept hard into my skirt and huddled like everyone else. I was thirsty, exhausted, and worried for my fate.

Later that day, the door to the common room opened, and the bailiff bellowed, "Mrs. Holloway!"

I scrambled to my feet, my heart beating wildly, my limbs cramped from sitting on the cold stone floor. I had no idea what was happening—was it time for my trial already? Or perhaps the magistrate simply wanted me back so he could make a few more jokes at my expense.

I found, to my astonishment, that the person the bailiff took me to in the jailer's room was James, the lad who worked for

Daniel. Still more astonished when James said, "I'm to take you home, Mrs. Holloway. You won't stay here another minute."

I had no words, not to thank James, not to ask questions. As I stood like a mute fool, James took my hand and pulled me from the jailer's room, through the courtyard, and out the formidable gate into the light of day. Or at least a rainy afternoon.

The area around Newgate was a busy one. James had to walk me through the bustle a long way before he pushed me into a hansom cab in Ludgate Hill.

I finally found my tongue to ask questions, but James did not enter the cab with me. He only slammed the door and signaled the cabby to go. I craned my head to call out to him as the cab jerked forward, but James gave me a cheerful wave and faded into the crowd.

Had Daniel rescued me? I wondered. If so, where was he? And why wasn't James coming with me?

James had said he'd been sent to take me home. What did he mean by *home?* Sir Lionel's house would go to whoever inherited the baronetcy—a younger brother, nephew, cousin. If his heir did not want a cook who'd been arrested for murdering the previous master, then I had no home to go to.

The cab took me, however, directly to Portman Square, and Sir Lionel's house.

CHAPTER 5

Daniel waited for me on the stairs that led down to the scullery. He ran up them with his usual verve to assist me from the hansom, then he paid the cabby and took me down into the kitchens.

I was shaking with hunger, worry, and exhaustion. I was grimy and dirty, my clothes filthy. A long bath, a hearty meal, and a good sleep would help me considerably, but I had not the patience for any of those.

I broke from Daniel and faced him, hands on hips. "Explain yourself, Mr. McAdam."

In spite of my bravado, my voice shook, my weakened knees bent, and I swayed dangerously.

Daniel caught me and steered me to the stool where I'd sat sharpening my knives the night Sir Lionel had come down. As I caught my breath, Daniel found the kettle, filled it with water, and set it on the stove, which had already been lit.

"Nothing to explain." Daniel moved smoothly about, collecting cups and plates from the cupboards, and rummaged in the pantry for leftover seed cake and a crock of butter. He knew his way around a kitchen, that was certain. "James told me you were in trouble, and I went along to see what I could do."

"But I was released," I said, trying to understand. "No one is released from Newgate. No one like me, anyway."

"Ah, well, the magistrates were made to see that they had no reason to keep you. The fellow who examined you is a fool, and the charge of murder has been dismissed."

I stared at him in astonishment. Daniel poured water, now boiling, into a teapot. He brought the pot to the table, and when the tea had steeped a few minutes, poured out a cup and shoved it and a plate of buttered seed cake at me.

"Get that inside you. You'll feel better."

Indeed, yes. I fell upon the feast and made short work of it. Soon I was no longer hungry and thirsty, but I remained half-asleep and filthy.

"What did you do?" I asked. "I sent Anne to find you, but I thought perhaps you'd do no more than see I had a solicitor, if that."

Daniel finished off his tea and poured himself another cup. "If you mean Anne the actress, yes, she did find James—James is a friend of her son's. But James had already seen you being arrested from here. He followed you to Bow Street and realized you were being taken off to Newgate. After that, he legged it to me and told me all. I regret you had to stay the night in that place, but I could not put things in motion sooner. I am sorry."

I listened in amazement. "You mystify me more and more. Why should you apologize, let alone rush to my rescue? *How* did you rush to my rescue? I'm only a cook, not a duchess, with no one to speak for me."

Daniel lifted his dark brows. "Are you saying a cook should be tried and condemned for a murder she did not commit, because she is *only* a cook?"

I was too tired to argue with him or even to understand what he was saying. "How do you know I didn't murder Sir Lionel? It was my knife in his back."

"Which someone other than you took from this kitchen and used. Someone evil enough to push the blame onto to you." Daniel sat down, comfortably pouring himself a cup of tea. He pulled a flask from his pocket, tipped a drop of whiskey into it, then a drop into mine, if you please.

He went on. "If you *had* killed Sir Lionel, why would you leave the knife in him instead of cleaning it up or getting rid of it? Why would you go happily back to bed to wait for the constables to arrive instead of running away? It was you who raised the alarm and sent for the police, wasn't it?"

"Yes." I had done all that. It seemed so long ago now.

Daniel sipped his tea, and I took another drink of mine. Whatever spirits he'd poured into the tea danced on my tongue and warmed my gullet.

Daniel watched me over his cup. "Tell me about these people who came to dinner with Sir Lionel last evening."

I could barely remember. "Mrs. Watkins would know better than I about his guests. She served at table, because Copley was a mess."

"Mrs. Watkins doesn't seem to be here. In fact, the staff have deserted the house. Does Mrs. Watkins have another address?"

I clattered my teacup to its saucer, my hands shaking. "Mrs. Watkins has a sister in Pimlico—Sally, the scullery maid, told me she'd gone there, if I remember aright. However, if you imagine I can give you the particulars of all the people who worked here and where they might be, along with the names and address of the friends who visited Sir Lionel last night ..." I broke off, no longer certain where the sentence had been taking me. "You clearly have never been up before a magistrate and thrown into a common cell at Newgate for a night. It clouds the memory."

"Oh, haven't I?" Daniel's dark eyes twinkled. "But that's a tale for another day. Come along, Kat. You have a good rest, and we'll talk when you wake."

I found myself on my feet, again supported by Daniel. "I'm wretched dirty. I need a wash."

"I have plenty of hot water going on the stove. Off we go."

He steered me to my little bedroom and then went back out to carry in steaming water and pour it into my basin. Daniel left me to it, saying a cheerful good-night.

I was so exhausted I simply stripped off every layer of clothing I wore and dumped them on the floor. I washed the best I could, then crawled into bed, still damp, in my skin.

Some believe it is very wicked to sleep without clothes, but I'd already been a sinner, and I couldn't see that God would care very much whether or not I pulled on a nightgown. I was asleep as soon as my head touched my pillow, in any case.

When I woke, it was bright daylight. I spent some time trying to convince myself that everything that had happened to me had been a bad dream, and that I'd rise as usual and go out into my kitchen to cook. I had an idea for tea cakes with caraway and rosemary that I wanted to try.

I threw back the covers to find myself unclothed, which reminded me of my quick bath, after which I'd been too tired to don a nightdress. This told me my adventures had been real enough—I was usually quite modest and would never risk being caught without any sort of clothing on my body.

The events of the night before notwithstanding, I rose and did my toilette, put on a clean frock and apron, pinned up my unruly hair, and set my cook's cap on my head. The familiar routine comforted me, and besides, I had no idea what else to do.

When I opened the door, the sharp smell of frying bacon came to me. I moved out to the kitchen to find Daniel at the stove, cooking. The urchin, James, a bit cleaner than he usually was, sat at the kitchen table.

When I looked at James this morning, I noticed something I had been too distracted to note in the past—he and Daniel had the same eyes. But then, I hadn't seen the two together when James's face hadn't been covered with dirt. Now I saw that the shape of James's jaw, the jut of chin, the manner in which he sat sipping a mug of tea, mirrored Daniel's almost exactly.

"You're his son," I exclaimed to James. I had no idea whether this fact was a secret, but I was too bewildered and tired to guard my tongue.

James gave me his good-natured look, and Daniel glanced over his shoulder at me. "Ah, Kat," Daniel said. "Awake at last. You slept the day away, and a night."

I rocked on my feet, disoriented. "Did I?"

"Indeed. I didn't have the heart to wake you yesterday, but I knew you'd be hungry this morning. Sit down—these eggs are almost finished."

"You have changed the subject," I said. "As usual when you do not wish to answer. Why did you not tell me James was your son? Why did *you* not tell me?" I shot at James.

James shrugged. "Embarrassing, innit? For me, I mean. T' have to admit *he* sired me?"

"I don't see why," I said. "You could do much worse than Mr. McAdam."

James grinned. "Suppose."

Daniel shot him a weary look, which made James more amused. I realized they must banter like this all the time. It reminded me of the jokes I shared with my daughter, and my heart squeezed.

By habit, I brought out my bin of flour and the sponge starter I kept on a shelf beside the icebox. I stopped after lugging the flour bin to the middle of the table. Who was I baking for? Did I still even have employment? And why were Daniel and James here, when no one else seemed to be?

"Where is everyone?" I asked. "Did Mrs. Watkins return? Copley? Sally?"

James answered, Daniel still at the stove. "The house be empty. Dangerous, that. Anyone could come in and make off with the silver."

"Have they?" I asked. "Was Sir Lionel robbed? And that's why he was killed?"

My hands measured the flour and bubbly starter into a bowl, and I took up a wooden spoon to mix it all together. The familiar feel of my muscles working as the dough grew stiffer calmed me somewhat. If there'd only be three of us today, I wouldn't need more than one loaf.

I stirred in the flour along with a dash of water and a smidgen of salt, then scraped the dough onto my table and began to knead. Neither Daniel nor James admonished me to stop. I'd refuse anyway—the vigorous kneading helped my agitation. I dumped the ball of dough into a clean bowl, covered it with a plate, and set it aside to rise.

As I wiped my floury hands, Daniel shoved a large helping of bacon and eggs at me. "Eat all that. Then we'll talk."

"Talk." I picked up the fork he'd laid beside the plate, suddenly hungry. James, likewise, was digging into the repast. "I think I never want to talk again. Perhaps I'll retire to the country. Grow runner beans and pumpkins, and bake pies the rest of my life."

"I'd eat 'em," James said. "She's a bloody fine cook, Dad."

"Watch your language around a lady, lad." Daniel scraped back a chair, sat down, and watched us both eat. He wasn't partaking and didn't say why, but I was beyond curiosity at this point.

Once I was scooping the last rom my plate and finishing off my second cup of tea, Daniel said, "Kat, I want you to tell me about the meal you served to Sir Lionel. Every detail. Leave nothing out."

"Why?" I came alert, able to now that I had a bit more inside me.

Daniel laid his hands on the table, giving me a kindly look, but I saw something watchful behind the compassion. "Just tell me."

It was the same gaze I often found myself giving him. Wanting to trust him, but knowing so little about him I was not certain I could.

"There was nothing wrong with my meal," I said firmly. "Was there?"

James frowned across at his father. "What are you getting at, Dad? You're upsetting her."

"Sir Lionel didn't die from the knife thrust," Daniel said, far too calm for the dire words he spoke. "That wound was inflicted post mortem. Sir Lionel had already been dead, though not for long, of arsenical poisoning. His guests, Mr. and Mrs. Fuller, also suffered from poisoning. Mr. Fuller died in the night. Mrs. Fuller, her doctor says, has a chance at recovery, but he can't say for certain whether she will live."

CHAPTER 6

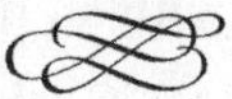

I sat staring for a full minute, perhaps two, my mouth hanging open. James looked no less astonished than I did. James had helped me with that meal, not only cleaning the fish and fowl but laying out ingredients for me, learning to chop mushrooms, and stirring up dough.

"No arsenic could have been in *my* supper," I said, when my tongue worked again. "They must have come by the poison elsewhere."

Daniel shook his head. "The coroner who examined the body said that the poison had entered the stomach at the same time as your meal. I'm sorry, Kat. You must take me through every dish. Please."

"Well, it could not have been in my food, could it?" I said in rising worry. "You brought me most of the ingredients that night, and I taste everything. If arsenic had been slipped into the sauces in my kitchen, it would have killed me too. And all the staff. I always hold a portion back to serve with our supper."

"Tell me," Daniel said gently.

I heaved a sigh. I could barely remember my name let alone

everything I'd made that fatal evening, but I closed my eyes in recall.

"A cream of leek soup. Whitefish with a velouté—a thickened broth and wine sauce. A salad of greens with a lime dressing and tart apples, asparagus with boiled eggs, roasted squab stuffed with peppercorns with a red wine sauce. A fricassee of mushrooms. There wasn't time for rolls with all this, so I made savory scones instead. For pudding, a thin chocolate soup to start, then custard tart with whatever berries I could find and a burnt sugar sauce. Copley chose the wine for me—perhaps *he* put poison in the wine, for whatever twisted reason he had. He's a villain; I've always said so."

Daniel shook his head. "There was nothing in the glasses, or the bottles. The coroner worked all night, testing everything he could."

"How do you know all this? Was there an inquest?"

Daniel shrugged. "He told me. He's a friend of mine."

Daniel McAdam, friends with a coroner. Why was I not surprised? "But how did he find the wine glasses?" I asked. "And the wine? Sally scrubbed everything and put it away."

"Not the wine glasses. She'd left them. The wine was still open in the butler's pantry. The police took all this away while you were ... detained."

The prison came back to me with a rush. I pinched my fingers to my nose, willing it away. When I opened my eyes, I found Daniel looking at me with such sympathy mixed with self-chastisement that it made me a bit dizzy.

I drew a breath, continuing the argument to stop the wild thoughts in my head. "The poison could *not* have been in the food," I said. "I told you, I taste everything before I allow it to go up, and every person downstairs had a helping of what every person upstairs ate. And we're all hale—well, I am, and James here appears to be."

"We're looking for the other staff," Daniel said. "We'll know soon enough."

I fixed him with a stern look. "If the coroner believes the cook poisoned the entire dinner party then why am I not still in Newgate?"

"Because of James," Daniel said, unworried. "If you had poured a box of arsenic into any of your dishes, James would have seen. You could, I suppose, have built yourself an immunity to arsenic so it wouldn't hurt you, but I know James did not. And he's not sick at all."

No, James was very healthy indeed, and listening with interest. He asked the question that was next in my mouth. "Why do you want to know all about the food, then, Dad? If you already know she didn't do it?"

Daniel opened his hands on the table. "To decide which dish might best conceal it, and how it was served. The wine and peppercorn sauce, the mushrooms, and the burned sugar on the pudding interest me most. They could have disguised the taste."

I only watched him, bewildered. "But who would have introduced this poison? I place the dishes in the lift myself. Are you saying you believe someone very small was hiding in the dumbwaiter with a vial of poison? Or something as nonsensical? Or do you believe Mrs. Watkins did it, or John, as they served the meal? Sally went nowhere near the food at all—she was busy washing up all my pots and pans."

"I can rule out none of them," Daniel said.

I blew out my breath. "I cannot imagine why on earth Mrs. Watkins, John, or Sally would do such a thing. None of them are mad, I don't think."

"They are not here either," Daniel pointed out. "Once you were taken away, John disappeared, as did your scullery maid, as well as your butler and several choice bottles of wine."

"Of course," I said in exasperation. "Copley took the wine to sell, no doubt—he refuses to drink the stuff himself. I imagine the others didn't return because they thought they had no place here anymore. Sally was terrified and fled before I was even arrested."

"Perhaps," was all Daniel would say. "Would it be too much for you, Kat, to cook the same meal, as you did that night? So I can see exactly how it was prepared?"

At the moment, I never wanted to cook anything again. But I heaved a sigh, climbed to my feet, and went through the larder to see what foodstuffs I'd need.

I had everything but the mushrooms, berries, fresh fish, and birds. James was dispatched to procure those. The leftover greens were a bit wilted, but edible, apples drying, but again, usable.

I set everything out as I remembered. A bit difficult because I never cooked to an exact recipe—I knew what went into each dish from experience, then I threw in a bit of this or that I had on hand or left out things I did not, so each meal was unique. A long time ago, when I'd first been a cook's assistant, I'd doggedly learned every step of a recipe and followed it religiously, until a famous chef I met told me to trust my own instincts. After that, my skills rose quickly.

I tried to remember what I'd done as I worked. I set Daniel to helping me chop leeks and greens, core the apples, stir the roux for the velouté, and cream the butter for the scones.

Daniel proved to be quite skilled at cookery, though it was clear he'd never handled a chef's knife before. I had to show him, with my hand over his, how to chop the leeks. His skin was warm, his breath on my cheek, warmer.

I might have stayed in the circle of his arm for a while longer had not James come banging back in. I nearly cut myself scrambling away from Daniel, who moved the knife safely aside, his eyes alight with amusement.

I set Daniel to washing and chopping the mushrooms, and James competently cleaned the fish in the scullery.

We created the meal again, which took the rest of the day, and then partook of it, enjoying the lightness of leek soup, the savory fish, the tenderness of the game birds with peppercorns, the sweet and tart tastes in the salad. The scones came out light and crumbly, the custard creamy with the bright bite of berries to finish.

When we ended the meal, Daniel pushed back his plate, clattered his fork to it, and let out a sigh. "You are an artist, Kat."

"It's only a bit of cookery," I said modestly, but I was pleased.

James wiped his mouth with the napkin I'd given him. "'Tis bloody hard work. All that, and you eat it in ten minutes."

"*You* eat it in ten minutes," Daniel said with fatherly fondness. He took a sip of the wine I'd brought out of the butler's pantry for the peppercorn sauce.

Daniel seemed to know about wine—he didn't quaff it but savored it, pronouncing the vintage excellent. He was a paradox, was Daniel, though I had long since discarded the belief that he was a simple delivery man.

"You do well in the kitchen," I told James. "You learn quickly and have a feel for the food. Perhaps you could study a bit and become a chef."

"A chef?" James snorted. "Cooking for pampered gentlemen who complain when their dinner hasn't been boiled long enough? No, thank you."

"Well." Daniel leaned back in his chair. "There was nothing wrong with that meal. Plenty of opportunities for you to slip in the poison, and you too, James—and me—but if everyone in the kitchen ate of the dishes, and you and James are well, I cannot see how the poison came from the meal as you cooked it."

"Thank you very much," I said. "You might have taken my word for it before we did all that work." Not that I'd eaten so well in a long time. I suspected part of Daniel's motive had been to partake in an expertly cooked elegant meal, which I doubted came along for him very often. I'd rather liked cooking with Daniel—and James, of course.

Daniel and James obligingly helped me clean up. I expected

them, as men often did, to abandon me once the enjoyment was over, but James scrubbed plates and Daniel dried them with good cheer.

I told them to leave me after that. I had nowhere to go and would make do with my bed here tonight, but tomorrow, I'd look for other digs and a new place.

James departed, his pockets full of leftover scones. Daniel lingered on the doorstep. "Are you certain you'll be all right, Kat?"

"Not entirely." The kitchen was echoing without Daniel and James in it, the rooms above me, too silent. However, the street was busy and noisy, and the neighbors and their servants were near to hand. "I don't have much choice do I? But I am made of strong stuff, do not worry."

"Hmm." Daniel glanced at the ceiling, as though he could see the entire house above us. "Lock this door behind me then. I've already bolted the front door but keep the door at the top of the back stairs locked. And don't go out until morning."

His caution unnerved me. I felt the weight of the house above us, empty and waiting. I drew a breath and repeated that I'd be all right, and at last, Daniel departed.

I locked the kitchen door then scurried up the back stairs to the door at the top, its green baize tight and unblemished, as though nothing untoward had occurred beyond it. I opened the door and peered out into the cold darkness of the house.

I was too sensible to believe in spirits, but the shadows seemed to press at me. Sir Lionel had died here, alone and unpitied.

I quickly closed that door, locked it, and descended again to the kitchen, where I rechecked the back door and made certain none of the high windows were open. The kitchen was stuffy with the windows closed, but I'd put up with it.

I retired to bed, but I could not sleep for a good long time, as tired as I was. I kept picturing the rooms upstairs, dark, deserted, silent.

At last I did drift off, only to be woken by a loud *thump*. Then came a creak of floorboard above me. Someone was in the house.

I had a moment of panic, wanting to put the bedcovers over my head and pretend it hadn't happened. But I hardened my resolve and sat up.

Burglars must have broken in—empty houses were good targets, especially those belonging to rich men. Sir Lionel's heir would no doubt arrive to take possession soon, but until then, a house full of silver, wine, and other valuables was a sitting duck waiting to be plucked.

I wasn't having it. I sprang quietly out of bed, pulled on a blouse and skirt over my nightclothes and found my good, stout boots. I'd run for the constable who patrolled the street—never mind he'd had a hand in my arrest—and bring him in to the take the thieves.

As I left my tiny bedchamber and made my way through the short hall to the kitchen, I heard the burglar start down the back stairs.

Damn and blast. The entire expanse of the kitchen lay between me and the back door. I knew why they'd come down here—the master's collection of wine and much of the silver lay in the butler's pantry beyond the kitchen.

I'd have to risk it. Taking a deep breath, I scurried across the flagstone floor toward the scullery and the back door.

A dark figure leapt down the last part of the stairs and grabbed me before I could reach for the door latch—the door was already unlocked, I saw belatedly. I let out a scream. A hand clamped over my mouth and dragged me back into the kitchen. I fought like mad, kicking and flailing with my fists.

"For God's sake, Kat, *stop*!"

Daniel's voice was a hiss in my ear, and a second later, I realized it was he who held me. I broke away. "What the devil are you doing, frightening me out of my wits?" I asked in a fierce whisper.

"Shh." He put a finger to my lips.

I understood. Though it had been Daniel creeping down to the kitchen, someone was still upstairs, robbing the place.

"It's Copley," Daniel said into my ear.

I started in indignation. "That rat. We should run for the constable. Catch him at it."

"The police are already waiting outside. When he runs out with the goods, they'll nab him. He won't have any excuse or chance to hide."

I went quiet as the floorboards creaked again. I might have known. "What if he comes down here?" I asked.

"Then I'll lay him out and deliver him to the Peelers."

I liked the idea, but I had to wonder. "Why are you hand in glove with the police?"

Daniel's vague shrug was maddening, but I fell silent. We traced Copley's path across the ground floor above us until he disappeared into the rear of the house.

"The garden door," Daniel said in a low voice, no more whispering. "That's how he came in. He'll find plenty of the Old Bill waiting for him as he goes out."

The nearness of Daniel was warming. "How did you know he was here at all?"

"I was watching the house, saw him pass a few times. Then he nipped around the corner to the mews behind it. I told the constable to bring some stout fellows, and I followed Copley inside."

"You were watching the house?" I was befuddled from being jerked from a sound sleep and having Daniel so close to me.

Daniel gave me a nod. "I wanted to make sure all was well. I worry about you, Kat."

He looked at me for a long moment, then touched my chin with his forefinger, leaned down, and brushed a kiss across my lips.

I was too astonished to do anything but let him. Daniel

straightened, gave me a wry smile, and moved around me to let himself out the kitchen door.

A blast of cold air poured over me, but my body was warm where he'd held me. I touched my fingertips to my lips, still feeling the pressure of his soft kiss.

CHAPTER 7

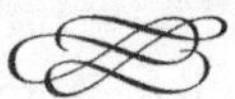

Daniel returned in the morning, knocking on the kitchen door, which I'd re-locked.

He'd brought James with him again, to help me with the morning chores necessary to any house, no matter I was its only resident. James whipped around, carrying in coal and helping stir up the fire, while I mixed up dough for flat muffins and fried the last of the bacon.

I kept glancing sideways at Daniel as we ate at the table, though he did not seem to notice. He said nothing about the adventure of the night before—not to mention the kiss—as if none of it were of any moment.

I was no stranger to the relations between men and women—I had a daughter, after all—but what I'd had with my husband had been sometimes painful and always far from affectionate. The gentle heat of Daniel's mouth had opened possibilities to me, thoughts I'd never explored. I'd had no idea a man could be so tender.

Daniel seemed to have forgotten all about the kiss, however. That stung, but I made myself feel better by pretending he was being discreet in front of his son.

After breakfast, I mentioned I needed to tidy myself and return to the agency to find another post, but Daniel forestalled me. "First we are visiting Mrs. Fuller."

I blinked as I set the plates on the draining board. "The woman who shared the fatal meal? She has recovered?"

"She has, and was lucky to. The coroner tells me there was a large quantity of poison in the two men, enough to kill a person several times over. Mrs. Fuller is rather stout, so perhaps the arsenic did not penetrate her system as thoroughly. Her doctors purged her well."

"Poor thing," I said. "Do you think Copley somehow added the poison to the meal? To clear Sir Lionel out of the way so he might help himself to the goods?" I contemplated this a moment, rinsing plates under the taps. "Perhaps he only pretended to be too drunk to serve that night, so the food wouldn't be connected with him."

Daniel shook his head. "I think Copley is more an opportunist than a schemer. Though he might have seen an opportunity to administer the poison and taken it."

"I still don't see how. Copley is limber and thin, but I can't imagine him crouching in the dumbwaiter shaft with a bottle of poison."

Daniel gave me his warm laugh. "Nor can I. Ready yourself, and we'll go."

James finished the washing up so I could change. I put on my second-best dress, the one I kept clean for visiting agencies or my acquaintances on my day out, or my occasional jaunt to the theatre. For church and visiting my daughter, I always wore my best dress.

This gown was a modest dark brown, with black piping on cuffs, bodice, and neckline. I flattered myself that it went with my glossy brown hair and dark blue eyes. The hat that matched it—coffee-brown straw with a subdued collection of feathers and a black ribbon—set it off to perfection.

Daniel gave me a glance of approval when I emerged, which warmed me. Ridiculous. I was behaving like a smitten girl.

But then, he'd never seen me in anything but my gray work dress and apron. James grinned at me, told me I was lovely, and offered me his arm. Sweet boy.

Mrs. Fuller lived on Wilton Crescent, near Belgrave Square. A fine address, and the mansion that went with it took my breath away. Daniel and I were let in by a side door, though James remained outside with the hired coach.

The ceilings of the house above stairs were enormously high, the back and front parlors divided by pointed arches. Plants were everywhere—we had stepped into a tropical rainforest it seemed. Rubber trees, elephant's ears, potted palms, and other exotic species I couldn't identify filled the rooms. The furniture surrounding these plants was elegantly carved, heavy, and upholstered in velvet.

The butler led us through the front and back parlors and into a bedchamber that looked out to the gardens in back of the house.

This room was as elegant as the others, the ceiling crisscrossed with beams carved like those in an Indian mogul's palace. Mosaics covered blank spaces in the ceiling, and outside in the garden, a fountain containing tiles with more mosaics burbled.

Mrs. Fuller lay on a thick mattress in an enormous mahogany bedstead with curved sides. Mrs. Fuller was indeed stout, about twice my girth, and I am not a thin woman. Her face, however, was pretty in a girlish way, the hair under her cap brown without a touch of gray.

I curtsied when the butler announced us, and Daniel made a polite bow. "I apologize for disturbing you, madam," Daniel began. "The police inspector thought Mrs. Holloway might be of assistance, as he discussed with you."

"Yes, indeed." Mrs. Fuller lifted a damp handkerchief from the bedcovers and wiped her red-rimmed eyes. "I am anxious to find out what happened. Forgive me, my dear, if I am not myself. It is still incredible to me that my dear husband is gone, and yet, here I am. You are the cook?"

"I am." I gave her another polite curtsy. "My condolences, ma'am. Yes, I cooked the meal, but I promise you, I never would have dreamed of tainting it in any way."

Mrs. Fuller dabbed her eyes again. "They told me you were innocent of the crime. I suppose you are suffering from this in your own way as well. Your reputation … you are an excellent cook, my dear. If it is any consolation, I so enjoyed the meal." Her smile was weary, that of a woman trying to make sense of a bizarre circumstance.

Daniel broke in, his voice quiet. "I've asked Mrs. Holloway about what she served and how she prepared it. It would help if you described the meal in your own words, Mrs. Fuller, and tell us if any dishes tasted odd."

Mrs. Fuller looked thoughtful. I pitied her, ill and abruptly widowed. She could have doctored the food herself to kill her rich husband, of course, but her husband dying did not mean she inherited all the money. That would go to her oldest son, if she had sons, or to nephews or other male kin if she did not. She'd receive only what was apportioned to her in the will or in the marriage agreement, though the heir could be generous and give her an allowance and place to live. However, the heir did not have to, not legally.

One reason not to marry in haste was that a widowed woman might find herself destitute. Careful planning was best, as were contracts signed by solicitors, as I'd learned to my regret.

"Let me see," Mrs. Fuller began. She then listed all the dishes I had prepared, forgetting about the mushrooms at first, but she said, "oh, yes," and came back to them. No, all tasted as they should, Mrs. Fuller thought, and she heaped more praise on my cooking.

"The custard at the end was very nice," she finished, sounding tired. "With the berries, all sweetened with sugar."

She had described what I did. Nothing added or missing. She and Sir Lionel had taken coffee, while her husband had been served tea, so if the poison had been in the coffee, she would have still have been ill but her husband alive.

Daniel seemed neither disappointed nor enlightened at the end of this interview. He thanked Mrs. Fuller, who looked tired, and we began to take our leave.

As her maid ushered us out of the bedchamber, a thought struck me. "A moment," I said, turning back to Mrs. Fuller. "You said the custard and berries were sweet with sugar. I put a burnt sugar sauce on the custard, yes, but did not sprinkle more sugar on top. Is that what you meant?"

Mrs. Fuller frowned. "I meant that there was sugar in a caster that came with the tarts on the tray. We all made use of it."

"Ah," I said.

Mrs. Fuller drooped against her pillows, the handkerchief coming up to her eyes again. The maid gave us a severe look, protective of her mistress, and Daniel led me firmly from the room.

I tried to walk decorously out of the house, but I moved faster and faster until I was nearly running as we reached the carriage.

"What the devil is it, Kat?" Daniel asked as he helped me in and climbed up beside me. "What did she say that's got you agitated?"

"The caster." I beamed as James slammed the door. "*There* is your incongruity."

Daniel only peered at me. "Why?"

"Because, my dear Daniel, I never sprinkle extra sugar on my custards, especially with the berries. Ruins the contrast—the custard is plenty sweet with the burnt sugar sauce, and the slight tartness of the berries sets it off perfectly. Extra sugar only drowns the flavor. I would never have sent up a caster full of it on a tray to ruin my dessert. I didn't, in fact. That means the poison must have been in the sugar."

Daniel's eyes lit, a wonderful sight in a handsome man. "I see. The murk begins to clear."

"Does it?" I deflated a bit. "Now all we need to know is where the caster came from, who put the poison into it, and how it got on the table that night."

Daniel gave me a wise nod. "I'm sure you'll discover that soon enough."

"Don't tease. I am not a policeman, Mr. McAdam."

"I know, but perhaps you ought to be." His amusement evaporated. "I must ask the inspector how he and his men missed a container full of poison when they searched the house."

He had a point. "The poisoner obviously took it away before the police arrived," I said.

"Oh, yes, of course. Why didn't I think of that?"

The wretch. My gaze dropped to his smiling mouth, and the memory of his brief kiss stole over me. If Daniel noticed my sudden flush, he said nothing, and we arrived at Sir Lionel's house again.

Nothing for it, but we began to search the place, top to bottom, for the sugar caster. I had to first explain to James what one was.

"A small carved silver jug-like shape, with a top," I said. "Like a salt shaker, but wider and fatter."

James nodded, understanding, but try as we might, we could not find it. We searched through the dining room, opening all the doors in the sideboard and the breakfront, then I led them downstairs to the butler's pantry.

The walls were lined with shelves that housed much of Sir Lionel's collection of silver, some of it handed down for generations through the Leigh-Bradbury family. Silver kept its value where coins, stocks, banknotes, and even paintings might become worthless. Heavy silver could at least be sold for its metal content if nothing else. Sir Lionel's plate had the hallmark of a silversmith from two centuries ago and was probably worth a fortune.

I discovered that at least a third of this valuable silver was missing.

"Copley," I said, hands on hips.

Daniel, next to me, agreed. "Meanwhile—no sugar caster?"

"If it's in this house, it wasn't put back into its usual place. Did Copley rush out of here with it in his bag of stolen silver?"

"Very possibly," Daniel said. "I will question the inspector who arrested him."

I became lost in thought. How likely was it that the poisoner had tamely returned the caster to the butler's pantry, ready for Copley to steal it? Unless Copley had poisoned Sir Lionel for the express purpose of making off with the silver. Why, then, had Copley waited until Sir Lionel had been found? Why not put the things into a bag and be far away when I'd stumbled across the body? The answer was that Copley most likely hadn't known that Sir Lionel would be killed. He was an opportunist, as Daniel said.

Daniel's shoulder next to mine was warm. I did not know what to make of him. Would I ever know who he truly was?

Well, I would not let him kiss me again and then disappear, leaving me in the dark. I was a grown woman, no longer the young fool I was to let a handsome man turn my head.

I voiced the thought that we should look for the caster in *un*usual places, and we went back to the dining room. After a long search, I spotted the sugar caster tucked into a pot containing a rubber tree plant.

The plant and its large pot stood just outside the dining room door, a nuisance I'd thought it, with its fat leaves slapping me across the back if I didn't enter the doorway straight on. As I impatiently pushed the leaves aside, I spied a glint of silver among the black earth.

I called to Daniel, and put a hand in to fish it out. He forestalled me, shook out a handkerchief, and carefully lifted it.

He carried the caster into the dining room, both of us breathless, as though the thing would explode. James fetched a napkin from the sideboard, and Daniel set the caster into the middle of it. With the handkerchief, he delicately unscrewed the top, then dumped the contents of the caster onto another napkin.

It looked like sugar—fine white sugar used to put a final taste on pastries, berries, cakes.

James put out a finger to touch the crystals, but Daniel snapped, "No!"

James curled his finger back, unoffended. "What is it?" he asked.

"Who knows?" Daniel said. "Arsenic, perhaps? Or some other foul chemical. I'm not a scientist or doctor."

"Or chemist," I said. "They sell poisons."

"True." Daniel wrapped the caster's contents in one napkin, the caster in the other, and put them all into the bag he carried.

"What will you do with those?" I asked.

"Take them to a chemist I know. Very clever, Mrs. Holloway."

"Common sense, I would have thought."

The teasing glint entered Daniel's eyes again. "Well, I have a distinct lack of common sense when I'm near you, Kat."

James rolled his eyes, and I frowned at Daniel—I refused to let him beguile me. "Be off with you, Mr. McAdam. I must put my things in order and find a place to stay. Another night in this house would not be good for my health, I think."

"I agree." Daniel gave me an unreadable look. "Where will you go?"

I had no idea. "I suppose I'll look for a boardinghouse that will take a cook whose master died after eating one of her meals. I'm certain I'll be welcomed with open arms."

Daniel didn't smile. "Go nowhere without sending me word, agreed?"

"Send word to where?" I looked him straight in the eye. "Your address, sir?"

Daniel returned my look, unblinking. "Leave a note here. I'll find it."

We continued our duel with gazes until finally Daniel gave me the ghost of a smile and turned away.

When James started to follow Daniel downstairs, I stopped him. "Where *does* he live, James?" I asked in a low voice.

James stuck his hands in his pockets. "Tell ya the truth, missus, I don't know. He finds me. He always seems to know where I am."

"And your mum?"

James shrugged, hands still in his pockets. "Never knew her. I was raised by a lady who chars for houses until he found me. But I've never stayed with him. I board with some people—respectable. He pays for it."

I was more mystified than ever. James behaved as though this were the normal course of things, though I saw a tiny flicker of hurt in his eyes that his father didn't want him rooming with him for whatever his reasons.

Daniel had banged out the front door. James rushed to catch up with him, and I closed and bolted the door behind them.

The house became eerier once they'd gone. I hastened down to my rooms, packed my things in my box, then left the box and went out again in hat and coat. I dutifully left a note for Daniel about where I was going on the kitchen table, which I'd cleaned and scrubbed after this morning's meal.

The first person I looked up was Mrs. Watkins, the housekeeper. She might have heard of a house looking for a cook, or might know where I could rest my head tonight.

Mrs. Watkins's sister lived in Pimlico. I found out exactly where by letting myself into the housekeeper's room and going through her small writing desk. Mrs. Watkins would have left all the paperwork and keys for the house for the next housekeeper, even if she'd gone in haste. I discovered everything neatly organized, as I'd thought I would.

I took an omnibus to Pimlico and found the house, a respectable address in an area of middle-class Londoners. Mrs. Watkins's sister, it turned out, ran a boardinghouse herself—for genteel, unmarried women, and Mrs. Watkins had just taken the last room.

"Mrs. Holloway!" Mrs. Watkins exclaimed in surprise when she entered the parlor to find me there. I'd asked the maid to send up word that Mrs. Watkins had a visitor, but I had not given my name.

"Good evening, Mrs. Watkins," I said.

"I heard ... I thought ..." She opened and closed her mouth, at a loss for words.

"Yes, I was taken before a magistrate, but then released." I made a dismissive gesture, as though I survived ordeals like being locked in Newgate every day.

Mrs. Watkins remained standing with hands clenched as she adjusted to this turn of events. "Well, I have to say I never thought you could have done such a thing. You have a temper on you, Mrs. Holloway, but plunging a knife into a man takes a cruelty I don't think you possess."

"The knife didn't kill him," I said. "He was poisoned. As were the others at the table. Now then, Mrs. Watkins, why did you set a sugar caster on the table when I didn't send it up with the meal?"

Mrs. Watkins gave me a perplexed frown. "What sugar caster?"

"The one Sir Lionel and his guests used to liberally sprinkle sugar all over my tart. Which they should not have—the flavor was just fine. If they'd known anything about food, those two men would be alive today."

Mrs. Watkins continued to blink at me. "You are making no sense. There was no sugar caster on the table."

"Then why did Mrs. Fuller say there was?"

"Gracious, I have no idea."

We eyed each other, two respectable-looking women standing in the middle of a carpet in a sitting room, the carved furniture and draped tables hemming us in. A lamp, already lit against gathering gloom, hissed as its wick drew up more kerosene.

The two of us were dressed similarly, our bodices tightly

buttoned to our chins. I wore a jacket of dark gray wool, while Mrs. Watkins was dressed in a simple ensemble for an evening indoors. She was tall and bony, I plump and shorter of stature.

No one could have mistaken us for anything but two ladies who'd had to grub for our living, except that we had a bit more responsibility and wisdom, and had left behind the lower levels of the serving class.

And yet, was that all we were—respectable women in the upper echelon of the servant class? Who really knew anything about us? I had a daughter but no sign of a husband. Mrs. Watkins—what had she been in life? Behind the layers we showed the world, what secrets did we keep?

"Are you certain there was no sugar caster?" I asked after a silence.

"Positive."

There it was. Either Mrs. Watkins lied, or Mrs. Fuller did. Was the liar the poisoner? Or did each of them lie for some reason I could not comprehend?

I needed an independent party to tip the balance. John the footman, Sally, or even Copley. John certainly would have seen what had happened at the table that night. He wasn't the brightest of lads, but he was worth speaking to—unless he'd done the poisoning, of course. And then there was Sally. She'd discovered Sir Lionel. Her fright and shock had seemed real enough, but I had been too stunned myself to pay much attention.

I thanked Mrs. Watkins, wished her the best, and left the house, pondering over what she'd told me. If she lied about not placing or seeing the caster on the table, why had she? I had no idea. What a muddle.

John proved to be elusive. According to Mrs. Watkins's notes, which I read back at Sir Lionel's house, he'd been a cousin of Sir Lionel's coachman, but that coachman had been dismissed before I'd been employed there. The coachman now drove for a banker with a house in Dorset. John had no other relation, it seemed, and

I had no idea how to go about looking for him. John might even now be in Dorset in search of a new position. Sally had a family in Southwark, the notes said, and I wondered if she'd retreated there.

I wrote a brief letter to the coachman who was John's cousin, addressed it in care of the banker in Dorset, and took it out to post.

Night had fallen. Streetlamps outside Sir Lionel's had been lit, and Portman Square teemed with people. London never really slept.

It was too late for the errand I truly wanted to run, so I began a brisk walk to a boardinghouse I'd lodged in before. Not the best, and the cook was deplorable, but needs must.

I had reached Oxford Street when I saw him.

Traffic blocked me from crossing, so I turned aside to buy a bun from a vendor. A little way behind me, a few well-dressed ladies and gentlemen were coming out of a large house and ascending into a coach.

One of the gentlemen was Daniel.

CHAPTER 8

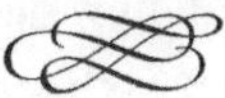

I was so astonished, I froze, the warm bun halfway to my lips.

Gone was the rather shabbily dressed man with heavy gloves and mud-splotched boots who argued in a good-natured way with his son. This gentleman wore a dark, well-tailored suit, which was clean and whole—in fact, it looked costly.

Creased trousers covered shining boots, and his overcoat against the evening chill fit him perfectly, made for him. A neatly tied cravat and a gold watch chain in his waistcoat completed the gentleman's ensemble.

Daniel's hair, instead of being its usual unruly mop, was slicked to flow behind his ears. He paused on the doorstep to set a tall silk hat on his head.

This couldn't be Daniel McAdam, could it? *My* Daniel?

My first inclination was to dart forward and look this person in the face. And if it were Daniel, ask him what the devil he meant by it.

I almost did. I hastily checked my steps, however, when I saw a woman emerge from the house and take his arm.

She was obviously a highborn lady. Her gown spoke of

elegance and refinement, silk and lace, with a glitter of diamonds at her throat. Not a courtesan, I thought. While courtesans could dress as finely as any lady, this gown was demure while also being highly fashionable.

A sister, I reassured myself quickly. Or a cousin. Something innocent. But the way Daniel handed the woman into the coach told me differently. He held her hand longer than was polite, helped her inside with a touch on her waist that lingered.

A sister might laugh at his care. This lady turned and gave Daniel such a warm smile that I nearly dropped my hunk of bread.

Daniel glanced around him, scanning the street in a surreptitious manner, as I'd often seen him do—assessing the lay of the land.

That glance clinched the matter. He was Daniel, and not simply a man who resembled him. His clothes were different, but his mannerisms, the look, the way he moved—Daniel.

As his gaze roved the street, I ducked back from the streetlight, earning me a growl from a passerby I nearly trod on. I begged his pardon and pushed myself into the shadows of a house, where the gaslight didn't reach.

I could scarcely breathe. Daniel finished scrutinizing the street and climbed up into the coach with the lady. The other lady and gentleman who'd come out of the house had entered the carriage as I'd watched Daniel. A footman from the house shut the door and signaled the coachman to go.

My heart was like stone as the carriage creaked away. I handed the uneaten bun to a beggar, drew my jacket about me, and walked on.

THE LANDLADY AT MY OLD BOARDINGHOUSE LET ME HAVE A SMALL room at the top of the house. It was cramped and cold, and I grew nostalgic for my cubbyhole behind the kitchen fireplace at Sir Lionel's.

It was not only the cold that kept me awake. I saw Daniel over and over in my mind, setting his fashionable hat on his head and touching the lady's back as he handed her into the carriage.

He'd been comfortable in those clothes, as comfortable as he was in his rough trousers and worn knee boots. He knew how to wear a gentleman's suit without awkwardness, and the lady with him seemed to find nothing amiss

Which was the real Daniel?

Or had I been mistaken? Daylight had been waning, gas lamps throwing a harsh glare on the street. Perhaps I had spied a man who had greatly resembled Daniel ... down to the turn of his head, the flick of his eyes, his way of looking about as though memorizing everything in sight.

The logical way to resolve the issue was to return to the house at Oxford Street, knock on the door, and demand to know if Daniel had been there last night. I had a good excuse to go to the house—I was a cook looking for a new position. Cooks didn't generally walk the streets knocking on doors, but it could happen. I would ask the domestics there about the household, perhaps make friends with their current cook, and discover what was what.

Another logical course was to ask Daniel point blank. That is, if I ever saw the man again and could strike up the courage to question him. I might not like the answers.

Or I could forget about Daniel altogether, visit my agency, find another place, and resolve to speak to him no more.

None of the scenarios satisfied me. I rose in the morning, cross and sandy-eyed, nibbled at the breakfast of undercooked bacon, overdone eggs, half-burned toast, and ice-hard butter, and went out. I wended my way back to Portman Square and Sir Lionel's, where all was quiet, to fetch my box.

I made certain that the kitchen and my room had been put to

rights—when Sir Lionel's heir took possession of the house I didn't want him blaming the previous staff for anything untoward. I'd need help shoving my trunk up the stairs outside, so I put on my hat with the feathers and black ribbon, and went out to ask the neighbor's boot boy to assist me.

I found James sitting on the scullery stairs. "Morning, Mrs. Holloway," he sang out.

I jumped. "James," I said, hand on my heart. "Good heavens, you should not do that."

"Sorry, missus."

I felt awkward speaking to him now. Did James know? Were James and his father deceiving me together, or did Daniel keep his own son in the dark as to whoever he truly was?

"No matter," I said. "You're just the lad. Can you help me with my box? I have a cart on the way …"

A cart pulled up in the street at that moment, and Daniel climbed down from it, his feet in scuffed boots landing outside the railings above me. I gulped and hastened back into the kitchen, not ready to encounter him just yet.

Daniel came ruthlessly inside. James darted past him to begin shoving my large, square trunk across the flagstones, but Daniel stood in the middle of the kitchen, his soft cap crumpled in his hand. His hair was its usual rumpled mess, his boots muddy, his loose neck cloth letting me glimpse a sliver of chest.

This was Daniel McAdam. The worker, unashamed of doing manual labor for a living. I had to have been mistaken about the other.

Daniel's good-natured expression was in place, as though he'd spent the night doing nothing more than drinking ale with his fellow delivery men in a public house.

"I thought you'd be agog to know what I learned from my chemist," he was saying.

I'd forgotten about the blasted chemist, and I *was* curious, drat him. "Did he discover what was in the sugar caster?"

"He did," Daniel said readily. "Nothing but sugar."

"Oh." I blinked, my thoughts rearranging themselves. "Then what was it doing in the plant pot? And why did Mrs. Watkins swear up and down that the caster hadn't been on the table at all?"

Daniel's gaze sharpened. "Mrs. Watkins, the housekeeper? When did she say this?"

"Yesterday afternoon, when I went to call on her. She's staying with her sister, Mrs. Herbert, who runs a boardinghouse. I believe I told you about the sister in Pimlico."

"And you went there to confront her alone?" Daniel's look was narrow and so angry that I blinked. "Without a word to me?"

"I left you a note." I pointed to the table, where the note had lain, though I'd put it on the fire this morning, no longer needed.

"You should not have gone alone," Daniel said sternly, his tone unforgiving. "You should have told me and had me come with you."

"To a ladies' boardinghouse?" I asked, my eyes widening. "They wouldn't have let you in. Besides, you had business of your own last night, did you not?"

Was it my imagination, or did he start? "I could have put any business off. This is important."

I had been avoiding looking straight at him, but now I lifted my chin and met his gaze.

"What *was* your business last evening?" I asked. "Did it take you to Oxford Street?"

Daniel focused hard on me as he went more still than I thought a human being could become. Everything affable about him fell away, and I was left looking at a man I did not know.

James and the neighbor's boot boy were pushing my box up the outside stairs—*thump, bump*—bantering with each other, laughing. Inside the kitchen, all was silence.

Daniel studied me with a gaze I could not read. No more warmth and helpful friendliness in his eyes, no more clever delivery man trying to find out who'd killed Sir Lionel. He was not even the cool gentleman I'd spied last night in Oxford Street. Daniel stood upright like a blade and looked as deadly.

"Then I *did* see you," I said softly.

His one, short nod lanced my heart. A rich gentleman did not pretend to be a poor one without ulterior reason—nor the other way around. Not very good reasons, either.

"The lady," I said, wanting to know the worst. "She is your wife?"

A shake of the head, as perfunctory as the nod. "No."

"Affianced?"

Daniel waited a bit before the next shake of head.

"Lover? I must admit, Mr. McAdam, I am quite curious."

"I know you are." His words were quiet, as were his eyes. "Mrs. Holloway, I have done you a great disservice."

He hadn't answered my last question. The knife in my heart twisted. "How so?" I asked. "By lying about who you truly are? I have known others who have done the same thing." The father of my daughter, for instance.

"I know."

It took a moment for me to comprehend those two simple words. *I know*. My beloved hat felt too tight on my head.

"What on earth do you mean by that?" I snapped. "You know what?"

Daniel's expression didn't change. "I know that the man who married you already had a living wife. That he abandoned you and left you to face the world alone, with a child. That you fought hard to gain the position you have. That you're a bloody good cook." The corners of his lips twitched as he said this last, but I'd never warm to his smile again.

"And yet," I said. "I know nothing about you."

"That is something I cannot remedy. Not yet. I regret that, Mrs. Holloway, believe me."

I noted that he no longer addressed me as *Kat*. "Well, I *don't* believe you. I was a fool ever to believe in you." I stopped the tears in my voice and cleared my throat. "Thank you for releasing me from prison, Mr. McAdam—or whatever your name is. Now, I must get on. I have to find another place so I may earn my keep, and my daughter's. Good day to you."

"I have already found another place for you."

I stopped in the act of pulling on a glove. "I beg your pardon?"

Daniel took a step toward me, cool and efficient. "The Earl of Clarendon, in Berkeley Square, needs a cook, one with excellent skills. You may start there anytime you wish."

Anger boiled through me, stronger than I'd felt in a very long time. How dare he? Daniel had caused me to make an idiot of myself, and now he sought to repair the damage by sending me off to the home of ... who? One of his dear friends? His relations?

"No, thank you," I said coldly. "I will go to my agency and see what is on their books. As is proper. Good *day*, Mr. McAdam."

"Kat, you need to take the position," Daniel said, his voice unyielding. "That and no other."

I thunked my small handbag onto the table. "Why? You tell me right now, Daniel. Why should I believe a word you say?"

His eyes flickered. "Because you will be safe there."

"*Safe?* From whom?"

"From those who wish you harm because of me." Every word was as hard as stones. "Sir Lionel died because of me. I did not kill him, but I caused his death. That is why I knew you never killed him—stabbed, poisoned, or otherwise, no matter what he'd done. When I learned he'd made advances to you, I warned him off and ensured that James or I watched you at all times. That is another reason I know you did not kill him—James or I would have seen."

I struggled for breath. "What are you talking about? *You* warned him off? What have you to do with Sir Lionel Leigh-Blasted-Bradbury?"

"Kat, believe me, I wish I could unburden myself to you, but I cannot. Not because I do not trust you, but because it wouldn't be safe for you. Or your daughter. Suffice it to say Sir Lionel mixed with people he should not have. In exchange for him continuing to live a free man, he was to tell me of all interactions he had with these people and the information they imparted to him. I believe that somehow, they got wind of what he was doing, and killed him."

"By poisoning my dinner?"

"By poisoning him *somehow*. I thought Mrs. Fuller had done so, making herself sick as a blind. But she was genuinely distressed and confused and grieving for her husband. I don't believe now she knew what dealings her husband had. The sugar caster ... I admit I have no idea how that fits in."

"I see." I said the words, but I saw nothing. I only knew that I had been made to think one way, when events had been something else entirely.

I could blame Daniel for deceiving me, but I mostly blamed myself. I'd been flattered by his attentions and preened myself because the handsome Daniel had interest in me.

"I thank you for explaining," I said, finishing drawing on my gloves. "I shall be boarding at Handley House in King Street, Covent Garden, if I can help you further in the matter of Sir Lionel. Good morning."

Daniel stepped in front of me. "I wish you to take the post in Berkeley Square."

His tone was firm, but I was tired of being told what to do. "No, thank you," I said. "I will find another position soon. I will send you word—somehow—of where if it will make you feel better."

I marched around him, straightening my hat as I went, and this time Daniel did not try to prevent me.

I went up the stairs without looking back, and to the street. I told James where I needed the trunk to be sent, and made my way to catch a hansom cab to take me to my boardinghouse.

After settling myself in there, I paid a visit to my daughter.

CHAPTER 9

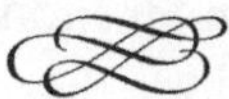

Once my so-called husband had vanished into the mists, and it became clear that I had never been legally married, I knew I'd have to work hard or my child would starve. Because I was unlikely to find a post as a disgraced woman with an illegitimate offspring in tow, I called myself by my maiden name—appending "Mrs." to it—and found a family who would foster my daughter.

The woman who took her in had been a friend to me since childhood. She'd been a kindly girl and was now a kindly woman. Her husband was good-natured and liked children, so my Grace lived with them and their four offspring in their tiny house and seemed to be happy.

Grace was never formal with me and unashamedly ran to throw her arms around me when I arrived. At ten years old, she was a beauty and possessed an understanding beyond her years. Grace did not resent the fact that I could not have her living with me where I cooked. She understood that we had to make our way in the world the best we could. One day, she said, she'd do the work and look after *me*.

I took her to walk with me in Hyde Park—our treat, after ices from a vendor. "Is everything all right, Mama?" she asked, slipping her hand in mine. Grace was always able to sense my moods.

I had not told my daughter about the horror of being arrested and imprisoned. I'd told my friend who looked after Grace but she'd agreed it wise not to mention it to the children, bless her.

"I am sad and confused, Grace," I said. "That is all."

"Because of the murder in Sir Lionel's house?"

So, she at least knew about that. Well, it is difficult to keep sensational news from a child, no matter how sheltered.

I admitted as much. "I will have to find another place. I'm not sure where it will be."

"I know *you* didn't poison anyone with your cooking, Mama," Grace said. "It must have been someone else."

"Yes, indeed. The puzzling thing is how." I pondered, forgetting to be cautious. "The arsenic was in no dish of mine. Mrs. Fuller said there was sugar; Mrs. Watkins says there was none. The sugar in the caster was tested—it was only sugar."

"Perhaps the caster was replaced with another," Grace said. "Afterward."

"An intriguing idea." I tapped my lower lip. "But why put the one with only sugar in the plant pot?"

"They meant to retrieve it later?" Grace, with her pointed face and fine hair, looked nothing more than a sweet-tempered child, but I knew what a quick mind her young face hid. "They meant to switch it for the clean one, but were interrupted. They didn't have time to fetch it out of the plant."

"Hm. A line I will have to investigate, I think."

"Will you tell me? If I'm right, will you tell me what happens?"

I squeezed her hand. "Of course I will."

We walked back to the omnibus and returned to my friend's home. My visit to Grace had lightened my heart. I never mentioned Daniel during this visit, and as I left my daughter, I realized he didn't matter. As long as I had Grace in my life, the attentions of deceitful gentlemen were of no moment to me.

I could not keep my thoughts entirely from Daniel, unfortunately, try as I might. As I made my way back to the boarding-house, I wondered anew who was the lady in Oxford Street, the one he'd claimed was not his wife. Was she another person Daniel was deceiving? Or was he watching her, as he'd done with Sir Lionel?

He'd said Sir Lionel had been meeting with certain people and reporting what they told him to Daniel, in exchange for Daniel ... doing what? Not telling the police Sir Lionel was spying, or plotting crimes, or whatever it was? Who were these bad people Daniel feared would hurt me? Or was *Daniel* the bad person, and whoever Sir Lionel had been in league with were on the side of good?

No, I couldn't believe that last. Sir Lionel had been mean-spirited, rather stupid, and cunning at the same time. He could not be up to any good no matter what he did.

Grace's idea about the sugar caster interested me, though. I could imagine someone at the table stealthily pocketing the caster full of poison, meaning to replace it on the table with one without poison. But they hadn't managed it and had to stash the clean caster in the plant. Because the people at the table had started feeling ill and rushed away? Or had the person trying to replace the caster been interrupted by John or Sally coming to clear the table?

But then, why had Mrs. Watkins claimed there was no sugar caster at all? Copley had been too drunk to wait at table that night ... or had he been? Had he crept upstairs and set the poison on the table, removing it again when Mrs. Watkins's back was turned?

There was nothing for it. I had to speak with Copley.

This entailed finding out where he was being kept, now that he'd been arrested for stealing Sir Lionel's wine and silver. I regretted hastening away from Daniel so abruptly, because Daniel would know.

I knew I'd never find Daniel if I wanted to—even if I waited outside the house in Oxford Street, there was nothing to say he'd return there—so I hunted for James. Sure enough, James was lurking around Sir Lionel's house with the excuse of doing odd jobs in the neighborhood. Daniel had told him to continue watching the place, he said.

When I told him I needed to speak to his father, James nodded and told me to wait inside Sir Lionel's house. He handed me the key, said he'd send Daniel to me, and ran off with the energy of youth.

I entered through the back door and went to the only place in that house I was comfortable, the kitchen. The familiarity of it wrapped around me, wanting to draw me back.

Too bad Sir Lionel had been such a terrible master. Perhaps when his heir moved in, he'd need a cook. The heir would be of sunnier disposition, appreciate my food, and not make strange demands on me or disgust me with amorous advances. Miracles could happen.

To pass the time, I went into the butler's pantry and looked through the silver in the glass wall cabinets. All was as it should be, except of course for the missing pieces that Copley had stolen. The settings all matched—the Leigh-Bradburys had used the same silversmith for years.

I frowned. I went to the housekeeper's room, fetched her keys, and returned to the pantry to open the cases. I studied the silver plates, candlesticks, and serving pieces like the chafing pan, a footed dish in the shape of a shell, the cruet stand, and a wine bucket. These pieces were larger, difficult to carry off without being noticed, which was no doubt why Copley had left them. Copley had taken smaller pieces—salt cellar, cups, spoons, finger bowls.

In a drawer below the glass-fronted shelves I found pots of silver polish and rags, as well as the velvet-lined boxes for the place settings. There were two unopened store-bought pots of polish with pink labels. A third pink-labeled pot had been opened, as had a pot of homemade polish—washing soda and salt, which the polisher would wet with lemon juice or vinegar before rubbing on the silver.

I took a delicate sniff of the homemade polish then closed the lid and slipped it into my pocket.

"Kat?" An alarmed voice was calling with Daniel's deep timbre. "Are you here? Where are you?"

I locked the cabinets, not hurrying, returned the keys to the housekeeper's room, and made my way to the kitchen.

Daniel breathed out when he saw me. "Damn it all, Kat ..."

"Please do not swear at me," I said calmly. "And I am *Mrs. Holloway*."

"Why did you have James find me?" The irritation and anger did not leave his voice.

"To take me to see Copley. I assume you know where they've put him?"

Daniel gave me a nod, his look hard. "At the moment, in hospital. He's seriously ill."

My brows lifted, my heart beating faster. "Oh, dear. In that case, I must speak to him at once."

Copley had been jailed at Newgate, but had been taken to the infirmary. He lay in a bed in a long, mostly empty ward. The ward was gray and unfriendly, windowless and gloomy, but it was a step better than the common cells. Just.

Copley looked terrible. His face was as gray as the walls and had a yellow cast to it. His entire body trembled, and when we approached, he turned over in his bed and vomited into the bucket at his bedside.

The air around him stank. I took a handkerchief from my bag and pressed it to my nose.

"Copley," Daniel said. "Sorry to see you so wretched, old chap."

Daniel was in his scruffy clothes again, holding his cloth cap. He looked like a carter or furniture mover, come to help the neat and tidy woman at his side. When we'd entered the jail, however, we'd been treated deferentially and led to Copley without question.

"What d'ye want?" Copley rasped. "Let me die in peace. Why'd ye bring *her* here?"

"You might not die," I said cheerfully. "Mrs. Fuller managed to recover. I imagine because someone politely replenished the sugar on her tart for her instead of making her shake it on herself. *You* probably only held the caster long enough to hide it in the plant pot, and luckily, you wore gloves."

Daniel glanced at me, perplexed, and Copley blinked. "What th' devil are ye going on about, woman?"

"It is simple," I said. "*You* took the sugar caster from the table." I pointed a gloved finger at Copley. "You did so when you thought no one was looking. Maybe when you and John were clearing up? Or John was clearing up while you helped yourself to any leftover food and drink." Those plates had been *very* clean when they'd returned to the kitchen. "You didn't have time to do anything with the caster—perhaps someone nearly caught you with it. Or you hid it when I sent John for the police and was downstairs dressing, fearing it would be found on you or in your room if there was a search. You stole many of the smaller pieces that night and stashed them to fetch later. Why not the sugar caster too?"

"Yes, all right," Copley growled. "I plucked the bloody thing off the table when I saw it, but Mrs. Watkins and John were right on top of me, so I hid it in the plant."

"Why not take it back downstairs with the other pieces?" I asked. I thought I knew the answer, but I wanted Copley to say it in front of Daniel.

"Because it weren't ours," Copley said angrily. "Not Sir Lionel's. I thought maybe them Fullers brought their own caster with them and forgot and left it behind. John would return it to our cabinet, not knowing the difference, then Mrs. Interfering Watkins would find it and send it back to Mrs. Fuller."

Daniel listened with a sparkle in his eyes. "You're saying the caster didn't belong in the house?"

Copley wet his lips, but he was losing strength, so I spoke for him. Copley really was a pitiful wretch.

"The sugar caster was made by a different silversmith," I explained. "If you check its hallmark, you'll see. Sir Lionel's family has used the same silversmith down the generations. All the pieces match. But I advise you, Mr. McAdam, that if you do handle the caster again, or your chemist does, please wear gloves. And ask your chemist to check the contents of *this*."

I brought out the small pot of homemade silver polish, which was still wrapped in my handkerchief. I set pot and handkerchief into Daniel's outstretched hands—which were covered with thick workman's gloves. He handled the pot with respect, but looked at me in bewilderment.

I turned back to Copley. "Did you or John ever use homemade silver polish?"

"No." Copley's voice was weak. "I used the stuff from Finch's. Much better for keeping off the tarnish."

"That's what I thought. Thank you, Copley. I do hope you mend soon."

"Would if the buggers in this place would give me a decent drop to drink."

I gave Copley a nod, pleased with him, and excited by what he'd told me. "That is possibly true." I said. "Shall we depart, Mr. McAdam?"

DANIEL INSISTED ON HIRING A HANSOM CAB TO TAKE US BACK through London. I didn't like to sit so close to him in the small vehicle, but rain had begun to pelt down, and I would have to endure the annoyance for a dry ride to King Street.

Daniel began speaking as though we had no tension between us. "You believe the poison was *on* the caster itself?" he asked. "Coating it?"

I nodded. "Test the homemade silver polish I gave you. If it were rubbed into a paste onto the caster, anyone lifting it would get it on their fingers. Then if they ate bits of food—eventually, they would ingest enough of whatever it is to make them ill. Or the poison could sink in through the skin. I'm not certain about that. Perhaps it would work by both means."

"Mrs. Watkins didn't take ill," Daniel pointed out. "If she handled the caster ... though she insists it wasn't there. What about poor John? We need to find him."

"John always wore gloves when waiting at table. Mrs. Watkins did not, but she was right as rain when I saw her yesterday, obviously not ill from poison. It is bad manners for ladies and gentlemen to wear gloves at table, and so the diners had no protection."

"But Copley?" Daniel frowned as he puzzled things out. "Why did it take him some time to become ill? Butlers wear gloves while they're setting up or serving at table, as footmen do."

He knew a lot about butlers, did he? "True, but I've watched how Copley sometimes takes his gloves off."

I demonstrated, delicately tugging at the fingers of one glove with my teeth, loosening it before drawing it off. "This is why I do not believe Copley poisoned Sir Lionel and the Fullers. If he'd coated the caster with poison, he'd have been more careful."

Daniel made a sound of agreement. "So, Copley is a thief, not a murderer."

This wouldn't help Copley much—he'd stolen items of high value and might be hanged for it, or perhaps transported if someone spoke up for him. Poor drunken fool.

"I will visit Mrs. Fuller again," Daniel said briskly. "And see if the caster came from her household. It is still possible *she* did the poisoning—or someone employed by her at her instruction."

I didn't think so, but I said nothing. Mrs. Fuller would have been certain to take the caster away and dispose of it, I would think, even if she'd deliberately made herself ill. The caster would not have been there for Copley to try to steal.

When the hansom stopped in front of my boardinghouse, I began to descend, but Daniel caught my hand and drew me back.

"I want you to take the post I spoke about," he said. "I will tell Clarendon's housekeeper to expect you for an interview."

I'd had enough. I jerked from his grasp but remained in the hansom. "Let me speak plainly, Mr. McAdam. You have deceived me at every turn. Believe me, I am vexed with myself for letting you. However, I have made my way in this world on my own for a number of years now, and I will continue to do so. I am grateful for what you have done for me—I sincerely thank you for saving me from the magistrates—but I have my life to get on with. I am not a silly woman; I will take every precaution for my own safety."

How this speech affected Daniel, I could not tell. He only regarded me with calm eyes—the eyes I'd once thought so handsome—and did not change expression.

"Very well," he said, his voice cool. "Then I will bid you good night."

I made a noise of exasperation. The least he could do was look contrite. He'd withdrawn, the affable Daniel gone, a cool shell in his place.

So be it.

My heart ached as I scrambled down from the hansom and made for my lodgings. I'd fallen for Daniel McAdam, whoever he was, but that Daniel did not exist. This was the painful truth I had to accept, and continue with my life.

CHAPTER 10

I saw nothing of Daniel or James for the next few days. I unpacked my box at the boardinghouse and visited my agency to find another post.

Difficult this time of year. Families of the big Mayfair houses were mostly gone to the country, and those who hadn't left already were packing to head out for the hunting and shooting seasons.

After that would be Christmas and New Years', the majority of society families not returning until spring. So many already had cooks installed in their London houses, cooks who went on preparing meals for the skeleton staff in the winter or for renters.

The minor gentry also went to the country or else they wanted a woman who'd plunk a joint of beef and watery potatoes in front of the family every evening and naught else. At least when Sir Lionel had been baiting me, he'd stretched my abilities and let me create meals worthy of a master chef.

I came away from the agency the days I visited it depressed and disgruntled. I might have to swallow my pride, hunt up Daniel, and take the post at Berkeley Square.

I did make a journey south of the river to see Sally, who had indeed returned home. She flew at me and hugged me, having believed me already convicted and hanged even in this short time. She was not much help, though. She knew nothing of the sugar caster or of the extra box of polish. She wasn't allowed to polish the silver, only to wash plates and crockery. The sugar caster never came near her sink, and she never went to the dining room or Sir Lionel's library.

She had nothing but honest innocence and confusion in her eyes, and I came away, unenlightened. She was about to start a new post in another kitchen, she said, thankfully. Her family needed her wages.

James arrived at the boardinghouse to visit me about a week after that. He did not actually come to the back door and request to speak with me; he simply skulked about in the street until I went out.

He told me with his usual cheerfulness that Daniel had found the footman, John, who was in Dorset, as I'd suspected. John was in raring good health, thank the Lord. Daniel had asked John to give him the gloves he'd used when serving that last meal and taken them away.

Daniel's chemist had tested the caster and found it coated with arsenic. That sort of thing could seep through the fingers or be eaten, with the same result—horrible illness and probable death. It could happen quickly, or take time—there must have been much of the stuff on the caster. Mrs. Fuller had indeed been very lucky.

When James finished giving me this news, I decided to ask him what I had been wondering about him point blank. "James, does it bother you that your father is not what he seems?"

The lad considered my question, his father's brown eyes in his smudged young face regarding me calmly. "I lived with the charwoman, as I said. She had a man also boarding in her house who wanted to use me as his fancy boy and beat me regular when I refused. One day, me dad—Mr. McAdam, as ye know him—came along, had the man arrested, and took me away."

James rubbed under his lower lip. "At the time, I thought me dad were the same—a man what liked boys, only he had a few more coins to rub together. But he got angry when I accused him of that. He told me he was my pa and would take care of me now. He showed me how we looked alike, and he knew all about my ma—may she rest in peace—and eventually, I believed him."

He shrugged. "Dad comes and goes all the time. I never asked where. If he has a posh house and family besides me—well some gents do, don't they? A house for the wife and one for the mistress? A house for his legitimate family, and one for his by-blows?"

I listened with mixed emotions. Daniel had been good to rescue James and make sure he was well looked after. On the other hand, James made a true point about gentlemen leading double lives.

"Thank you for telling me," was all I could think to say.

James grinned. "Don't look so primmed up, missus. I've always known I weren't the Prince of Wales. I'm a gent's bastard, Dad's kind to me, and I get by."

Would that I could take such a casual attitude. Daniel indeed led a double life—a triple one, perhaps.

However, I'd had my fill of men who did whatever they pleased, never mind who they trampled over or cast aside along their way, uncaring of how many women bore their children and were left to raise them on their own.

"Thank you, James, for telling me the news. I know you had no need to keep me informed."

"Thought you'd like to know. Dad said you'd be interested but didn't think you'd want to see him."

"He thought right." I dug into my pocket and pulled out a coin, but James lifted his hands and stepped away.

"Don't insult me now," he said. "I did ya a favor." He renewed his grin, tipped his cap, and jogged away into the busy London street.

When next I had the time, I made my way to Pimlico to visit Mrs. Watkins. Daniel might be questioning Mrs. Fuller and her staff up and down, but I wanted to quiz Mrs. Watkins again about that bloody sugar caster.

I met her in the sitting room of her sister's boardinghouse. She was having the same difficulty as I in landing a new post, but I imagined she'd find one before I did. More Londoners needed housekeepers while they were away than wanted to bother with cooks, especially cooks of my calibre.

"Perhaps I should open a restaurant," I said. "Though where I'd find the funds for such an endeavor, I have no idea."

"You'd soon tire of it," Mrs. Watkins said with conviction. "Instead of cooking for one table that complains, there'd be many tables complaining all night. My sister ran a restaurant for a time, but gave it up for a boardinghouse. An easier task, she says."

The maid brought tea, Mrs. Watkins poured, and we drank.

"Are you certain about that sugar caster?" I asked after we'd sipped.

Mrs. Watkins coughed, set down her teacup, and wiped her mouth with a napkin. "The one you asked me about before? Of course I am certain, Mrs. Holloway. I would have noticed it."

I took another sip of tea. The service was elegant, delicate porcelain with sprays of pink roses on it. No silver in sight, except for the small teaspoons. "You see, Mrs. Watkins, John says he saw the caster there. So did Mrs. Fuller. And Copley stole it, the wretch, hiding it to take away later. So you must have either been extremely unobservant, or are telling me an untruth."

"Well, you may believe what you like." Mrs. Watkins's indignation made her cup tremble as she picked it up again. "John is not bright, Copley only saw a silver piece he could steal, and Mrs. Fuller is obviously lying. *She* must have poisoned the meal, perhaps in the wine. They poured that themselves."

I sipped tea again and gave a little shrug. "It may be as you say."

"I will tell you what I think." Mrs. Watkins leaned forward, the cameo at her throat moving. "That delivery man, Daniel McAdam, as was always hanging about the house. He must have had something to do with it. There's something not quite pukka about him."

I nodded, saying nothing.

I had, in fact, considered Daniel as a suspect. He certainly was good at misleading. If he'd been watching Sir Lionel as he'd said, having Sir Lionel report to him, perhaps he'd begun to see the man as a danger.

Sir Lionel could report to these bad people that Daniel was requiring Sir Lionel to give him information. To shut Sir Lionel's mouth, Daniel poisoned the caster and got it to the table somehow—perhaps through Copley. When I was arrested for his deed, he felt remorse and decided to help me.

I had not pursued this line of thought, because my emotions about Daniel were jumbled, and I refused to trust my own judgment where he was concerned, at least not for the moment.

The maid brought in a stack of clean plates and began to lay them on the long table on the other side room. Tea would be served to the other tenants soon, and I ought to go.

I rose, but instead of leaving, I walked to the table. The maid was setting at one end a silver cream pot, sugar bowl with lumps of sugar in it, and sugar caster for the finer sugar that would be sprinkled on tea cakes.

I took up the caster, turned it over, and examined the hallmark, finding it identical to the one on the caster we'd found at Sir Lionel's.

The maid, ignoring me, moved to the other end of the table and laid out a twin of the cream pot and sugar bowl—two sets for a large number of diners.

I moved to her, lifting the second sugar bowl as though admiring it. "Do you have two of everything?"

"We do," the maid said, continuing to lay out forks and spoons. "It's not posh silver, but it's nice looking, I think. Except for the second sugar caster. That's gone missing."

I turned around to Mrs. Watkins, the caster and sugar bowl in my hand. Her face had become a peculiar shade of green.

"So the caster *didn't* come from Mrs. Fuller," I said to Mrs. Watkins. "It came from here."

A number of things happened at once. The maid looked up in surprise, her expression holding nothing but bewilderment. The door to the parlor opened and Mrs. Watkins's sister rushed inside. Mrs. Watkins left the sofa and came at me in a run.

Certain Mrs. Watkins meant to attack me, I held up my hands protectively, the silver pieces still in them. Her sister, Mrs. Herbert, came after her.

At the last minute, Mrs. Watkins swung around, putting herself across me like a shield. "Leave her be," she said swiftly. "Mrs. Holloway knows nothing. She'll say nothing."

I stared in surprise at Mrs. Herbert, the sister, and then realized that I'd seen her before—in a photo in Sir Lionel Leigh-Bradbury's library. She was older now—that photo had been of a fresh-faced young woman. I recognized the straight nose and regular features, the happy eyes of that girl. Now cynicism and age lined her face.

"Who are you?" I blurted out.

"I was his affianced," Mrs. Herbert snapped. "I broke the engagement when I realized what a parsimonious, evil little man he was. I married a better man. And then Sir Lionel ruined him. My Charles died in disgrace and penury, because of *him*."

Thoughts rearranged themselves rapidly in my head. Mrs. Watkins swearing the sugar caster hadn't been there, John swearing it had, and Copley plucking it from the table after supper and hiding it.

"You gave Copley the poisoned polish and told him he must use it, didn't you?" I asked Mrs. Herbert. "Paying him a nice sum for his services? I have no idea if he knew what it was—he might have been more careful if he did. Then you told Copley to carry the caster to the table. I shouldn't wonder if you promised him he could have it. If his greed made him ill or killed him, so much the better."

Mrs. Watkins, whom I'd never seen less than dignified, shook with tears. "Oh, Letty. How could you?"

"I have no remorse," Mrs. Herbert said, her head high. "Sir Lionel held a minor government post, and he filled enough ears with lies to have my Charles investigated for treason. The case dragged on and on until Charles sickened and died. He was proved innocent in the end, but too late for him. Sir Lionel killed my husband, as good as stabbing him through the heart."

"Is that why you stuck my carving knife into him?" I asked. "To make a point?"

Mrs. Herbert looked momentarily puzzled. "I never went into the house. Or near it."

Of course she hadn't. That way, nothing would connect her to the crime. The damning sugar caster would be taken away by Copley, cleaned and sold. No one would know it came from Mrs. Herbert's house.

But Copley had bungled it, lost his nerve, possibly when John had come to clear the table, and stuffed the caster into the rubber tree's pot to be retrieved later. He'd been caught going back into the house to find it and the other pieces he'd stashed, while the poison was working inside him to make him sick.

I could picture Copley creeping up to Sir Lionel's library, where the man sat, dead already, to stick my carving knife into his back to both ensure the man was dead and throw blame upon me. The scullery maid had heard him moving about and came to fetch me, so Copley had to flee back upstairs and pretend to be just waking up, no time to pick up the caster.

And then the house had been full of police, rambling all over it for the next day or so, and Copley had made himself scarce to wait until the house was empty again. He couldn't have known that I'd be released from prison and Daniel would be watching to catch him.

"How could you?" Mrs. Watkins repeated. "A second man died, and his wife was taken ill."

"Copley is ill as well," I put in.

Mrs. Watkins went on, ignoring me. "Any of us in that house could have touched that piece or used the polish, Letty. John, the scullery maid, Mrs. Holloway, even me."

Mrs. Herbert scowled. "Would serve you right for working for that monster, taking his money."

"I did it for *you.*" Mrs. Watkins began to sob. "I was trying to discover how to ruin him. For you!"

Mrs. Herbert paused at that, then her expression hardened. "I am not sorry that Sir Lionel is dead. My Charles has been avenged."

With that, she came at me in a rage. Mrs. Watkins caught her sister before she could reach me. I was about to spring forward and give Mrs. Herbert a good thump, when the woman's heel caught on the carpet, and she collapsed to the sofa.

The strength went out of her, her face growing pale, her pupils narrowing to pinpricks. Her breath came in gasps, full-blown hysteria on its way.

Mrs. Watkins sank down beside her sister, crying as well, the two of them becoming a wailing mess. The maid looked on in shock.

I put down the silver pieces, opened my bag, removed my smelling salts, and went to the two ladies, waving the little bottle under their noses.

Mrs. Watkins sat up abruptly, but Mrs. Herbert remained slumped against the sofa's back, breathing hard. I could see the innocent beauty she'd been before she'd been trapped by Sir

Lionel. Sir Lionel had been an odious man, and I couldn't help believe he'd been justly punished.

On the other hand, there was nothing to say Mrs. Herbert wouldn't simply become a crazed poisoner. She'd not worried a bit about the rest of us being sickened as well, from the Fullers—people she'd never met—to her own sister. In addition, I'd almost been tried for the crime, my fate, certain hanging.

I took from my bag the vial of laudanum I'd brought for the purpose of subduing Mrs. Watkins—because I'd thought it she who'd poisoned Sir Lionel and the Fullers. While Mrs. Herbert lay gasping like a fish, I held her nose and poured the laudanum into her mouth, forcing her to swallow.

Mrs. Watkins was still crying, but she made no move to stop me. Perhaps she too worried that her sister had gone a bit mad.

After that, I strode out of the room and out of the house, in search of a constable. I nearly ran into James, who was hovering near the railings that separated the house from the street.

"Gracious, what are you doing here?" I asked him.

"Following you," James said. "Dad told me to. You all right?"

"No. Fetch a constable, will you? I've found the poisoner of Sir Lionel Leigh-Bradbury."

I had the satisfaction of seeing young James gape at me before his face cleared, and he beamed.

"I knew you could do it!" he shouted, then was away in a flash, running to find the nearest constable.

CHAPTER 11

I was never certain what happened to Mrs. Herbert. She was arrested, likely shut in to the same kind of cell I had been, her trial scheduled.

I walked away from Mrs. Watkins, her house, Sir Lionel's, and all the rest of it. I visited my daughter again, holding her close until I could breathe once more.

I knew, though, that I'd never be free of it in my heart. I'd lived in a house where a man had been poisoned and died, and I'd condemned a woman to death for it. She'd go to the crowded cell in Newgate where I had waited in fear, only she would not be set free.

I'd met Daniel, half fallen in love with him and had been sorely deceived by him. After Grace's father deserted me, I'd vowed I'd never let a man trick me again, and yet the first fine pair of eyes I saw, I was off. I badly needed to curb these tendencies.

My agency did at last find me a post a few weeks later, in a large house in Richmond. The lady of the house had heard of my cooking from my previous employer, Mrs. Pauling, and was happy to have me.

Richmond was a bit far from my daughter for my taste, but the pay was good, I had an ample number of days out, and it was only a short train ride to the heart of London. Perhaps I could bring Grace out to Richmond to visit me, and we could walk along the river and see the sights. She'd like that.

The house was a good place, with the kitchen run efficiently—even more so once I'd taken command.

One cold winter day, as I went over a list of what I needed to prepare supper, a gentleman walked, unannounced, into the kitchen.

This house had a large servants' hall across the passage from the big kitchen, its own laundry rooms, housekeeper's parlor, a butler's pantry far larger than the closet-sized one at Sir Lionel's, and a fairly cozy bedroom down the corridor for me. The corridor and rooms were always teeming with the servants needed to tend a large household.

The gentleman could only have entered the servants' area by coming down the stairs that led to the main house, or in through the scullery door from outside. Either way, he'd have been noticed and politely questioned by the three strapping footman, the butler—who was a proper butler and not a wastrel like Copley—and the housekeeper, long before he reached the kitchen.

However, no one seemed to have stopped him, and the entire staff, when I looked around, was startlingly absent.

The gentleman was Daniel. He was dressed in what I would say were middle-class clothes—not so posh as the ones I'd seen him wear in Oxford Street, but not so scruffy as his work trousers and boots. His hair was tamed but not pomaded, a bit rumpled, but combed flat. He set a hat and pair of leather gloves on my kitchen table and rested one hip on the tabletop as though perfectly at home.

"It is good to see you, Kat."

I waited a few heartbeats until I was certain my voice would not crack. "Good day, Mr. McAdam. How is James?"

"He is well. Working." A wry look entered his eyes. "That is, when he's not off doing what he bloody well pleases."

"Ah." I knew Daniel wanted me to smile, so I did not. "What brings you to Richmond?"

"Hope." Daniel's gaze fixed on me. "I want us to be friends again, Kat. Like before."

"Oh, do you now?" I laid down the list of foodstuffs and clicked the pencil next to it. "Well, I'm certain *you* would feel much better if I agreed. If I forgive you, you will be much relieved."

Daniel lost his forced, polite look. "Damn it, Kat."

He came to me and pulled me around to face him, holding my arms with his hard hands. I felt the solid lip of the table behind me as I looked up into his angry face. Daniel's eyes had a dangerous glint in them. I had no idea what he was about to do, but I lifted my chin.

"Threatening me will not help your cause," I said crisply. "Remember, I'm a dab hand with a knife."

Rage turned to frustrated amusement. Daniel cupped my face with a firm hand, leaned down, and kissed my mouth. "I could fall in love with you, Kat Holloway," he said, his voice low.

My heart fluttered like a dove's wings. However, I refused to let him know that I could fall stupidly in love with him in return.

"The lady in Oxford Street might be a bit put out," I said. "Mr. McAdam dallying with a cook? Not the done thing."

Daniel made an impatient noise. "The lady in Oxford Street is —was—an assignment. Like Sir Lionel. Both of those are finished."

"Are they?" My heart beat thickly, and I could barely think. The kiss had been a rather fine one, Daniel stood close, and my coherence was running away. "You should be on to the next thing then."

"I am. Unfortunately. But I had to ..." Daniel trailed off, his fingers on my face softening. "I wanted to make sure you were well, Kat."

"I am," I said, surprised my voice was so steady. "As you can see. This is a fine kitchen."

"It is." Daniel drew a breath, lowered his hand, and deliberately stepped away from me. "What is it you prepare tonight, Mrs. Holloway?"

I had to consult my list, because my menu had just gone clean out of my head. "Beef bourguignon. Sorrel soup, fish in white wine, and lemon tart to finish."

"Ah, Kat, you make my mouth water." Daniel kissed his fingers to me, slanting me his wicked look. "If I happen to be passing in my delivery wagon after supper, might I beg a scrap or two to sustain me?"

He wanted to transform back to the Daniel I knew best, did he? "What about this?" I asked, waving my hand at his suit. "This … banker's clerk, or whatever you are? Where will he be?"

"Gone after this evening, I'm afraid."

"I see. Will I ever, perchance, meet the real Daniel McAdam?"

Daniel lost his smile. "Perhaps one day. Yes, definitely one day, I'll bare my soul to you, Kat. I promise."

My voice went quiet. "Will I like what I see when you do?"

"I don't know." The words rang true. "But I believe I am willing to risk it."

I had no idea what to say to that, or what I ought to do. Forgive him? Turn my back on him forever? Do neither, and go on with him as though nothing had happened?

One thing was certain—there was far more to Daniel than met the eye. I was curious enough, blast it, to want to learn everything I could about the man.

"In that case," I said, taking up my pencil again. "If you are not too late, I might save back a bit of lemon tart for you."

Daniel's smile returned. "I would enjoy that very much."

We shared a look. Daniel took up his hat and gloves, giving me a bow.

"You have more skills than cooking," he said. "Perhaps you will help me on another hunt someday."

I shivered. "Indeed no. Once was enough for me."

"Was it?" Daniel carefully pulled on his gloves. "We'll see. Good afternoon, Mrs. Holloway. I look forward to speaking with you again."

And I, you, I wanted to say, but held my tongue. "Good afternoon, Mr. McAdam."

He shot me a grin, came back to me, kissed me on the lips, and strode out, whistling.

AUTHOR'S NOTE

A Soupçon of Poison was one of the first historical mysteries I wrote —or at least started to write. I found the opening chapter for this novella stuck in a file in a box when cleaning out my flooded house. I enjoyed the chapters and remembered my plans for the characters of Kat and Daniel, so I dusted off the story (literally), wrote the rest of it, and published it.

Because of the great response from readers to Kat Holloway and Daniel McAdam, I decided to continue her series as I'd planned to do before my writing career went in a different direction.

Kat's adventures continue in the full-length novel, *Death Below Stairs* Book 1 of the Kat Holloway Below Stairs mysteries. Kat has her own website as well:

www.katholloway.com.

All my best,

Jennifer Ashley

MRS. HOLLOWAY'S CHRISTMAS PUDDING

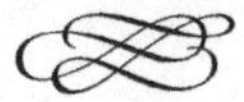

INTRODUCTORY NOTE

Events in *Mrs. Holloway's Christmas Pudding* tale place between Book 6, *The Secret of Bow Lane* and Book 7, *Speculations in Sin*. It features Kat and Daniel, Lady Cynthia, Mr. Thanos, Tess, and more.

CHAPTER 1

December 1882

"Mr. Whitaker is very ill." Mrs. Bywater's words rang through the kitchen as my young assistant, Tess, and I cleaned up from supper and began preparing for tomorrow's breakfast. "What on earth did you put in the plum tart, Mrs. Holloway?"

I turned abruptly, my fingers floury from the bread dough I'd been mixing.

Cooks were often the first to be blamed when a dinner party guest fell sick. Mrs. Bywater's words stung me all the more, because a few years ago I had been accused of actually murdering an employer, though with a carving knife, before the details of the case had become known.

No matter what, such an allegation must be nipped in the bud.

"He did not grow ill from my cooking," I said firmly. "I test every dish before it goes up, and Tess tastes them too. There was nothing wrong with the food."

"And yet, my husband's friend Mr. Whitaker became quite sick and had to be taken home to be looked after by his doctor," Mrs. Bywater snapped. "Mrs. Whitaker is at her wit's end."

"I cannot help that, madam," I replied, striving to keep my temper. "If the gentleman is ill, it has nothing to do with my meal."

I spied Mr. Davis, the butler, who had entered the passageway outside the kitchen. As he stood behind Mrs. Bywater, he let outrage show on his face. He did not like servants being the first accused either.

Tess's freckled face darkened, and I feared she'd pipe up in my defense. Tess had a very frank way of speaking, and her runaway tongue might get her dismissed.

We were interrupted by a click of heels in the corridor, and the next moment, Lady Cynthia Shires, splendid in a gray gown trimmed with black, swept into the room.

"Absolute nonsense, Auntie," she said loudly. "Mrs. Whitaker herself says Mr. Whitaker's doctor has treated him for weakness over the past few years. Besides, if Mrs. Holloway's cooking had been the culprit, we'd all be rolling about in agony."

I winced at her blunt way of putting it, but Cynthia had a point. One person was unlikely to eat the only tainted bite in a whole dish.

Mrs. Bywater pressed a hand to her slim waist. "I have been feeling a bit dyspeptic myself. I am certain it was the plum tart. Should have boiled those plums first, Mrs. Holloway, and in any case, kept them back for the Christmas pudding."

I pressed my lips together to rein in a sharp retort. We'd had an excess of the fruit, which Mrs. Bywater had found at an agreeable price and spontaneously ordered several crates of. Plenty for the plum puddings for Christmas and New Year's, she'd said.

In vain had I pointed out that "plum" pudding didn't actually have any plums in it. Currants, raisins, citrus peel, and other dried fruits, yes—these held together with plenty of breadcrumbs, suet, spices, and brandy.

Mrs. Bywater said my notions were silly, and of course we'd have plums in the Christmas pudding.

As she was mistress of the household, I'd ceased arguing. I'd been trying to use up the plums in other ways, but Mrs. Bywater complained every time I served them that I was wasting them. Not that she didn't eat an entire bowlful whenever they were put in front of her.

Though she consumed her food heartily enough, Mrs. Bywater was of a slender stature, with graying dark hair twisted into a simple knot. Her light-brown eyes stared into mine with the stubbornness of one who will not be told she is wrong.

"Mr. Whitaker's illness came from elsewhere," I repeated. I had a stubbornness of my own. "A sherry before his arrival tonight, perhaps. Or his afternoon tea."

Mrs. Bywater gazed at me as though I were a simpleton. "It was never his tea, or his sherry. What a notion. Find out which dish was responsible, Mrs. Holloway, and throw anything left of it into the slop pail. I suppose it won't even be fit for the dogs the coachman insists on keeping. If it was the plums, wash them and boil them down before you use any more."

I should have curtsied and agreed to obey, but my legs refused to bend. I knew full well my preparations had nothing to do with any illnesses, though I also knew Mrs. Bywater would never believe me.

Mrs. Bywater gave a jerk of her head, as though finding me impertinent and defiant. "You should have more care for what comes out of this kitchen, Mrs. Holloway. Else you might have to find another to work in."

Dealing that blow, which made my heart thump in fear and anger, she turned on her heel and tramped out of the kitchen. We listened to her stride down the hall to the back stairs and up them, every step emphasizing her disapprobation.

Once the door at the top banged shut, Mr. Davis stormed into the kitchen.

"Mr. Whitaker was already ill before he began to dine," he said in irritation. "Hobbled in, dabbing at his forehead with a handkerchief, and groaned all the way through the meal. I hope he didn't give anyone in the household his ague."

"Mrs. Whitaker told us her husband's digestion was delicate," Cynthia said. "Didn't stop the man from stuffing himself with everything on offer. Probably doesn't eat half so well at home. Auntie tucked in quite thoroughly herself. If she's dyspeptic, it's because she laced herself too tightly before gorging."

"Is Mr. Whitaker so very ill?" I asked, concerned.

"Yes, poor chap," Cynthia answered. "He had to be carried out by two of the footmen and put into his carriage. Mrs. Whitaker is quite worried. It's too bad—I rather like the man."

Life was precarious, and a chill or fever could carry one off without warning. Even if Mr. Whitaker was in the last stages of consumption, however, Mrs. Bywater would find a way to blame me. It was an ongoing battle between the two of us, Mrs. Bywater ever seeking an excuse to be rid of me.

"I will need to find out exactly what happened," I decided.

"We know it's nothing to do with you," Cynthia said quickly.

I appreciated her loyalty, but her friendship wouldn't help if Mrs. Bywater sacked me, which she likely would if Mr. Whitaker died.

If I lost my post, it would be a disaster. Most of the salary I earned went directly to my friends, Joanna and Sam Millburn, for the keeping of my daughter. If I had no way to pay Joanna, the Millburns might not have the wherewithal to look after Grace.

Cynthia knew this, as did Tess, though Mr. Davis did not. An unmarried cook with a daughter was not the sort of person Mrs. Bywater would let remain in her employ, so I had sworn Cynthia and Tess to secrecy.

I suppressed a sigh. "I will simply have to prove to Mrs. Bywater for once and for all that none of my dishes were tainted."

Very annoying as I was especially busy with preparations for the upcoming Christmas dinner. Mrs. Bywater had decided the family would stay in Town this year, with Cynthia's family traveling up to see her, instead of she going to them. I was glad of Cynthia's presence, because I liked her and missed her when she went to her father's estate, but it did mean more work for me and less time I could spend with Grace.

"Why should you have to prove it?" Mr. Davis began, jerking me from my thoughts, but Cynthia interrupted him.

"Because Auntie won't leave off until Mrs. Holloway has thrown away every morsel in the house, which is ridiculous. She would then complain about the expense of replacing it all."

"Course, we'd be rid of all them plums," Tess murmured behind me.

Cynthia acknowledged this with a grin. "I'll help, Mrs. Holloway. Glad to."

She was kind to me, this fair-haired, blue-eyed earl's daughter who defied convention, befriended a cook, and went about with her friends dressed in gentlemen's suits. Her eccentric ways couldn't hide a good heart or a quick mind, and I was forever grateful she had come into my life.

"Thank you," I said with sincerity. "I'll need to know exactly what Mr. Whitaker ate, and also what sort of illnesses he suffers from."

"I can help with that." Cynthia bounced on her toes in her restlessness. "Round up all your friends, Mrs. Holloway. We'll rush about for you. Won't we?"

She directed the question at Mr. Davis and Tess. Tess agreed eagerly, and Mr. Davis gave her a conceding nod.

"I will list the dishes he partook of," Mr. Davis said. He turned and glided from the room, his footsteps quiet as he made his way to the butler's pantry.

"*All* your friends, Mrs. H." Cynthia's eyes danced. "Will you send for him, or shall I?"

It wouldn't be as easy as Cynthia surmised to locate Daniel McAdam, the person to whom she'd been referring to when she'd said *All your friends.* Daniel had been in Ireland until recently, doing secretive things for the man he worked for, an icicle of a being called Mr. Monaghan.

It was by no means certain Daniel would answer my summons. He sometimes disappeared for long stretches at a time, doing who knew what for his guvnor. I did not know if I'd even need his help. He was good at catching those who set off incendiary devices and tried to assassinate the queen, but Mr. Whitaker's illness was hardly in the same league. But I welcomed Daniel's thoughts on any problem and supposed it did no harm to send word to him.

Once Cynthia went upstairs, I took my basket of scraps out to the beggars who habitually came to stand in the shadows in Mount Street. They knew I would emerge to dispense the leftovers at a certain hour every evening. I didn't worry they'd take sick from them, because as I'd said to Mrs. Bywater, Tess and I ate a little of everything, so we'd discover if something was off.

The tall young man with Daniel's eyes was there and gave me a cheerful greeting. I asked him to tell his father I wished to speak to him. James agreed with his usual energy and bounded off after he accepted the small piece of plum tart I'd tucked into his hand.

I decided there was no sense in me waiting for Daniel this evening, so I finished my chores, sent Tess to bed, and retired myself.

There was also no sense in me fretting too much about Mr. Whitaker. A man with a weak constitution having to be taken home and put to bed likely had nothing to do with what he had or hadn't eaten that day. Mr. Davis had given me, before he'd gone to bed, a list of all the dishes Mr. Whitaker had consumed, which had been most of them. Everyone else had eaten the same, he told me. I'd thanked Mr. Davis, the information confirming my own convictions.

Some people could not stomach certain foods, it was true. I always tried to provide a variety of dishes at dinner parties so those with a sensitivity could find something of which they could partake.

Nonetheless, I was always most careful with my ingredients, making sure all were fresh as could be before I put them into any of my dishes. I could sleep with a clear conscience on that note.

Even so, I tossed restlessly and returned, sandy-eyed, to the kitchen in the morning.

Surely Mr. Whitaker would have recovered from his distress by now, I reasoned as I began to prepare breakfast. He'd be fine after a night's rest, wouldn't he?

The best way to discover what was happening in another house in Mayfair was to ask the servants. Tess, who was a friendly chatterbox, had plenty of mates in the neighboring houses of Mount Street, South Audley Street, and beyond. It did not take much doing to send Tess on an errand where she could strike up a conversation with another maid on a similar errand. Through the gossip that permeated Mayfair, she soon returned with an answer.

"Mr. Whitaker is still powerfully ill," Tess announced as she set a basket of greens and winter vegetables on the table. "The family lives in Brook Street, so my pal Sally says. At Number 18. She's friendly with the cook's assistant there, name of Agnes. Mr. Whitaker was insensible when they brought him home and is still in his bed. His doctor has been there all night, and Mrs. Whitaker is certain they'll be laying him out in no time. She's sure someone poisoned him."

I did not like the sound of that, but I forced myself to resume my confidence. "Well, he was not poisoned here. As Cynthia stated, everyone at the supper would have taken sick if he had been, and the two of us as well."

"Stands to reason, don't it?" Tess agreed. "As far as I've heard,

Mrs. Whitaker ain't blaming Mrs. Bywater and her dinner party, but she's still convinced someone fed her husband poison of some sort. His doctor fears he won't recover. Such a shame," Tess continued with sympathy. "And so close to Christmas too."

She had a good heart, did Tess. "Please speak to your pal whenever you can," I instructed as I sorted through the produce she'd bought. "And let me know if there's any change in Mr. Whitaker's condition." If Mrs. Whitaker was correct, and there was a poisoner lurking in Mayfair, I wanted to know about it.

"Right you are, Mrs. H. I found some lovely parsnips." Tess took up two pale carrot-shaped vegetables and waved them about. "Can we roast 'em with them potatoes you have for tonight's supper? I know they'll taste ever so nice."

THE REST OF OUR DAY WAS TAKEN UP WITH THE USUAL PREPARATIONS for meals for the family and staff. Mrs. Bywater inserted herself into the larder at one point, asking if I'd thrown out everything from last night's meal, and I had to reassure her that all was gone. I was quite relieved when she went upstairs again.

I was still out of sorts when Lady Cynthia bounded down the outside stairs not long after the midday meal went up, her nose twitching in excitement. She was dressed in a gentleman's suit, which she wore when she visited her more unconventional friends.

"Your aunt believed you'd be home for luncheon," I warned her. "Several of her friends came to discuss books with her."

Cynthia seated herself at my table. "Too busy to put on a frock and fuss. I doubt the ladies have actually read the books in question, in any case. I wager they tell each other what they've read *about* them and don't bother to open the covers. A tedious afternoon avoided. I say, do you have a scone or something of the sort I can feast on?"

I knew Cynthia sought refuge here for a quick meal out from under her aunt's watchful eye. I rounded up a few currant scones with some lemon curd and blackberry jam, and threw in a slice of plum tart for good measure.

Cynthia, as always, had a robust appetite. She made quick work of the food, licking her fingers clean of jam as I told her what Tess had reported to me this morning.

"Yes, Whitaker is in a bad way," Cynthia said when I finished. "I've asked some of my chums who know the family about him. Tess has the right of it. My friends tell me that Mrs. Whitaker is convinced her husband's been poisoned."

"It's a bit strange she is insisting on it," I said as I brought out the parsnips to slice. "When a husband has been dispatched by poison, it is usually the wife who is the first suspect."

"I thought of that." Cynthia skimmed lemon curd from her scone and sucked the bright yellow paste from her fingertip. "She was sitting nowhere near him during dinner. In fact, *I* sat across from Mr. Whitaker. Auntie seemed to think he'd be impressed by an earl's daughter." She scoffed. "He was not, though he tried to be jolly about being saddled with me. I could tell he was unwell. He looked a bit pasty."

"Who else was near him?" I asked, eager for more details.

"His wastrel nephew, Herbert," Cynthia replied. "Herbert stands to inherit Mr. Whitaker's fortune if Whitaker pops off."

"Oh," I said, intrigued. "And was he sitting next to Mr. Whitaker?"

"No, indeed." Cynthia widened her eyes. "Auntie would never let two gentlemen sit together at her table, or two ladies either. Horrors. Whitaker was flanked by two of Auntie's friends who nattered at him like mad. Again, he was polite and made the best of it. The wastrel nephew was one seat down from him. I suppose Herbert could have dropped a dollop of poison into one of the dishes that was being passed around. Of course, there'd be no certainty that Mr. Whitaker would be served the poisoned dose."

"No," I agreed. "Much too complicated. What I imagine is that Mr. Whitaker was given the poison—if indeed it is poison—before he ever entered this house."

"That makes much more sense. Whitaker did arrive with his wife and the nephew, so either of them could have slipped a jolly good dose of arsenic into his sherry. There's also a friend, a Mr. Hardy. Apparently, he owes Whitaker a vast amount of money."

A desperate person wanting to get out of debt made an excellent suspect. The nephew was a good prospect as well. I laid aside the parsnips, pulled my notebook from my pocket, and began to scribble with my stub of a pencil.

"Is there anyone else in his life who might be happier with him out of it?" I asked.

Cynthia, finished with her repast, rocked back in the chair. "I'm not sure. I put the question to Judith, who knows everyone in London. She and Bobby are back from Paris, by the way—well, obviously, since I spoke to them."

She referred to her friends Miss Judith Townsend and Lady Roberta Perry. I'd asked them to help me with a problem not long ago, and on my advice, they'd gone to Paris to finish the business.

"Was their journey fruitful?" I asked, perking up a little.

"Indeed." Cynthia's eyes sparkled. "Judith is most grateful to you."

"I am glad," I said, pleased Miss Townsend had found what she'd sought.

"Anyway, Judith believes Whitaker has a ladybird tucked away somewhere," Cynthia went on. "That is something to find out."

"I would think the ladybird would want him to stay well and healthy." I scribbled another note. "If he dies, she's cut off, isn't she? Unless he has a remarkably generous will."

"No idea," Cynthia said, surprisingly cheerful for someone discussing potential murderers. "Ah, here's McAdam."

CHAPTER 2

My pencil cut a jagged swath across the page as Cynthia unceremoniously announced Daniel's arrival.

I had not seen much of Daniel since his return from Ireland. He'd delivered a bag of salt to my kitchen a few weeks ago, which had been his way of telling me he was back in London. After that, his visits had been fleeting and never when he could speak to me alone.

Here he was now, handsome in his patched coat, neckcloth carelessly knotted about his throat. He'd removed his cap from his thick dark hair, letting the hat hang negligently from his fingers.

I watched him note the position of everyone in the room—Tess peeling potatoes, Elsie washing up from the luncheon, Cynthia tilted back in her chair, and the footmen scrubbing silver across the passageway in the servants' hall. He didn't blatantly glance about, but he quietly made certain he knew who could hear anything said in the kitchen.

"Afternoon, Mrs. Holloway." Daniel gave me brief nod and Cynthia a deeper, more deferential one. "Your ladyship."

He also had greetings for Tess and Elsie, and he waved at the footmen, who happily looked up from their tasks to grin back. Daniel had time for everyone.

"To what do I owe this honor, Mr. McAdam?" I asked primly as I set aside my notebook and began to slice the parsnips. One would never guess he'd kissed me good-bye, most passionately, before his departure for Ireland.

"Happened to be passing." Daniel gave me an affable shrug. "Wondered if you had any orders for me. Something you need to stock? I can find you all the best foodstuffs, you know."

He winked as he played the part of a deliveryman who was trying to drum up business—he did a little selling of goods on the side.

"Nothing today, I am afraid." I answered in the tone of cook who didn't like to be coaxed into purchasing more than I needed. "Another time, Mr. McAdam."

I knew full well Daniel's question was to convey that James had told him I was asking for his help. My answer meant I couldn't speak to him about it now and that we should meet later.

"Did you hear how one of the master's guests was poisoned?" Tess blurted out. "He's ever so ill, and the mistress is blaming Mrs. Holloway."

Daniel's gaze shot to me, concern filling his eyes. He'd understand how distressing this would be for me, though I hoped this time I'd not land in Newgate.

"I told Auntie it was all rot," Cynthia said. "We're trying to work out who gave him the poison, if anyone did at all."

"I wager it *were* his wife," Tess said. "Angry about his ladybird."

"That is enough gossip from you," I told her severely, but I was pleased she'd broached the subject. I might have had to wait for days before Daniel could visit me in private.

"We are back to why Mrs. Whitaker would announce he'd been poisoned if she'd done it herself," Cynthia said. "She'd be safer to say that it was another manifestation of his ongoing illness."

"Unless she wanted to shift the blame to someone else," Tess suggested, ignoring my command. "Probably the ladylove. Two birds with one stone. That's what I would do."

"Would you?" Daniel asked Tess teasingly. "I ought to warn your Constable Greene then."

Tess flushed. "Caleb's all right. He'd never dream of having a ladybird."

I knew a bit more than Tess about the male sex, and yes, it was perfectly possible for any of them to stray. Men had so little control of their yearnings in that direction. The more virtuous a man proclaimed himself, the more adept he was at hiding his sins.

I admitted that Caleb Greene, the constable who walked our street, was a good lad, earnest and kind. I prayed he remained so, for Tess's sake.

"I would like to hear what the doctor has to say." I set the slices of parsnip on a plate. "I doubt he'd speak to a cook about his patient, but it would be helpful to know what poison he might suspect. Something easily obtainable?"

"Or something more obscure, like a rare snake venom?" Cynthia asked in excitement. "Thanos might be able to help there, Mrs. H. He can talk about compounds and concoctions no one else but another scientific mind would understand."

Mr. Elgin Thanos lectured at the Polytechnic in Cavendish Square. He was foremost a mathematician, but he knew much about chemistry and electromagnetism and many other obscure subjects that were beyond my grasp. Cynthia assisted him most days, helping him prepare for his talks, writing things on the blackboard for him, and making certain he could find his books, pens, and bits of paper, and wore matching boots.

Mr. Thanos was also a kind young gentleman and a great friend of Daniel's, who had assisted us on many cases.

"I doubt it will be a rare snake venom," I said. "That only happens in stories and on the stage, does it not, Daniel? I mean, Mr. McAdam?"

Daniel shrugged. "Anyone can bring back strange substances from the far corners of the British Empire. But I agree, Mrs. Holloway. An untraceable poison isn't as likely as what can be found around a house. Arsenic and such."

"One must be very careful what one buys at the market," I said. "All sorts of powders might be used to fill in an order of flour. That is why I test all my food before it's served," I finished with indignation.

"Even so, Thanos can find out the particulars once we know more," Cynthia broke in. "The mum of one of my friends sees Mr. Whitaker's doctor—Dr. Burnley—about her ailments. I might be able to ask the man point blank about Mr. Whitaker's health or have my chum do it."

"If he is a proper doctor, he will not tell you," I said. "I believe it's bad form to discuss a patient."

"I'll wheedle it out of him then," Cynthia said with confidence. She leaned toward Daniel and spoke softly, "What about you, McAdam? Will you put on a disguise and quiz the family?"

Daniel chuckled. "No need, your ladyship. I deliver to many homes in Mayfair."

Cynthia looked disappointed. She found it much more fun when Daniel pretended to be a man of the City or an inane upper-class gentleman to do his investigations. I preferred him to remain himself.

A delivery man could go to any house and talk to the servants there, including those of the wastrel nephew and the ladybird. Even if the household hadn't ordered anything, Daniel could claim he'd brought the delivery by mistake and then charm the staff below stairs into giving him a cup of tea and a crumpet or two.

Speaking of that …

"I suppose you expect me to feed you," I said to Daniel. "You ever manage to turn up right after a meal, do you not, Mr. McAdam?"

Daniel rubbed his hands together. "Because I know I'll find the best food here. There are houses with cooks so unskilled I have to protest like mad to keep from eating what they offer."

His flattery pleased me, but I strove to hide it. "So that is the secret of why you visit me." I rose and clumped to the dresser to fetch him a plate.

Cynthia laughed at my feigned grumpiness. I spooned out a large slice of plum tart and dolloped a good portion of leftover Chantilly cream next to it.

"Have a care, McAdam," Cynthia said as I set the plate in front of Daniel. "That is the exact tart my aunt claims poisoned Mr. Whitaker."

Daniel forked up a large portion and slid the pastry through the cream. "Then I will die a happy man, your ladyship." He shoved the whole concoction into his mouth, smiling as he chewed.

"I always say you're a daft man, Mr. McAdam." I sat down, elbows on the table and sipped tea.

Daniel sent me a wink from his sparkling blue eyes, which warmed me all the way through.

I WAS NOT ONE TO SIT IDLY AND LET OTHERS ASK QUESTIONS FOR ME, especially when my livelihood might be at stake. After Daniel and Cynthia departed, I finished the preliminary preparations for that evening's supper and told Tess I was going out.

Shopping for goods, of course. A cook couldn't leave her place of employment on a whim, and my day out wasn't until tomorrow. Besides, that day was for Grace.

Brook Street lay a short way from the house in Mount Street. I walked to Berkeley Square, then headed north a few blocks on Davies Street, passing Brook's Mews before I turned to Brook Street itself.

I tucked my basket more securely under my arm and walked the length of the road, trying to appear purposeful. The street was not long, running from Hanover Square to Grosvenor Square, and I traversed it quickly. Number 18 lay near New Bond Street. The house had a portico with round columns between the pavement and the door, a relic from a past age.

Iron railings separated me from the stairs down to the kitchen. I peered into the recesses of the stairwell, wondering if I should boldly descend. The cook of this house would be familiar with Mr. Whitaker's digestion and what foods bothered him. I'd come here with the purpose of inventing an excuse to speak to her, but while I debated, someone ascended the stairs from the house next to the Whitakers' and paused to stare at me.

"Is it Mrs. Holloway?" a stout woman in a black hat with too many feathers asked.

"Mrs. … Cullen." I recalled the name from my encounters with this cook at the greengrocers. "Good afternoon."

"If you've come to have a chat, love, I'm off on my day out."

"Oh, I see." I strove to sound downcast. I'd known from our casual acquaintance that Mrs. Cullen worked in Brook Street but not in which house. She had often encouraged me to visit her when I had a moment.

Middle aged, with a round face under her out-of-date hat, Mrs. Cullen liked to talk. And talk. I'd avoided the visit knowing she looked for an opportunity to converse at length. I didn't mind letting a person chatter away to me, but not for several hours at a time. However, she was in a position to know much, if not all, of what happened in the house next to hers, especially if she spoke often with the Whitakers' kitchen staff.

"Thought I'd take the chance," I continued, lingering. "Oh, well."

"Walk with me a bit, if you like," Mrs. Cullen said. "I'm off to visit my sister, and I catch the omnibus at Oxford Street."

On any other day, I'd find an excuse not to stroll with Mrs.

Cullen while her jaw wagged with her many trains of thought, but this afternoon, I readily fell into step beside her.

"Terrible about Mr. Whitaker next door," I prompted.

"Isn't it just?" As predicted, Mrs. Cullen was off, happy of the excuse to tell me all. "Mrs. Whitaker is most distraught. She's telling all who will listen that her husband's been poisoned. Terrifying." She pressed a gloved hand to her ample bosom. "And me living right next door."

"I heard that Mr. Whitaker is a rather sickly man," I said.

"He is indeed, Mrs. Holloway." Mrs. Cullen began a litany of every ailment Mr. Whitaker had suffered from since she'd come to work in Brook Street three years before. He had poor digestion and a weak heart, and sometimes couldn't leave the house for days. Or he'd take a constitutional, all bundled up in coat, muffler, and wooly hat, so that a person could barely see there was a man inside at all.

"Why is Mrs. Whitaker convinced it's poison?" I asked, trying to sound in awe of Mrs. Cullen's observations.

"Because it came on sudden-like. He's been moaning and groaning, can't rise from his bed, their housekeeper says. Housekeeper's blaming the food at a house party they went to, but no one else from that meal has been sick, so Mrs. Whitaker claims." Mrs. Cullen sounded disappointed, as though she'd prefer to see everyone who'd dined at our table struggling to live this morning.

Mrs. Cullen appeared to have no idea that the dinner party in question had taken place at the house I worked in, and I did not enlighten her.

"Then it must be illness," I concluded.

"So says the doctor. He's our doctor too, and he's quite frustrated with Mrs. Whitaker. What does she know about poisons? he's asking. He's only seen the like of Mr. Whitaker's symptoms in true maladies."

"There must be some reason she is insisting," I said.

"*I* think she fed her husband the poison herself." Mrs. Cullen gave me a decided nod. "And is trying to push the blame onto Mr. Whitaker's nephew, Mr. Herbert, a young man who is good for nothing. Wears grand clothes, runs with an extravagant crowd, and is always touching his uncle for money. He inherits the lot if Mr. Whitaker pushes off."

"Perhaps *he* gave Mr. Whitaker the poison," I suggested. "Would he have had the chance?"

"Of course he would. Mr. Herbert is in and out of the house all time, runs tame there. The Whitakers never had any children. From what I understand, Mr. Whitaker could never come up to scratch." Mrs. Cullen spoke without embarrassment about the man's rumored infertility. "Mrs. Whitaker says she's not bothered —bearing a child is dangerous for a woman, isn't it? Mr. Herbert is a handful enough without her having to worry over children of her own, Mrs. Whitaker says. She's besotted with her husband, never thought of annulling the marriage to catch a man who could fill her nursery. I understand her point of view. I've never wanted a husband and little ones to be a slave to. Children are a nuisance, and we have a much easier time without them, don't we, Mrs. Holloway?"

I nodded dispassionately and inwardly apologized to Grace for pretending to agree.

When Grace had arrived in my life, I'd been terrified. I'd had no idea what to do with a tiny baby, though it was true Grace had been a sunny-natured infant. Without my friend Joanna's help I think I would have gone mad or fallen into deep despair.

Even so, I'd never trade Grace for the world. Her father, deceased now, had been an awful person, but he'd given me one good thing—Grace.

Not all women wanted children, I knew. It was a myth, usually voiced by men, that women were only fulfilled when taking care of husbands and nurturing children. This lofty idea ignored the fact that some husbands could be brutes. Likewise, that some women worked themselves to an early death trying to feed and look after their many children, which came courtesy of their brutish husbands. My life might have gone that way if Mr. Bristow hadn't gotten himself killed.

So, I both agreed with Mrs. Cullen that a woman needed more in her life than squeezing out children and disagreed that we were better off without them.

"Gentlemen like having sons to carry on their name," I ventured. "Mr. Whitaker is not bothered that he doesn't? Or perhaps he is but hides it well."

"He's looked upon his nephew as his own son since his brother passed on," Mrs. Cullen said. "The brother never had much in the way of money, and Mr. Whitaker has rather indulged Mr. Herbert, knowing he'd inherited nothing. But he's spoiled the young man. And this is how Mr. Herbert thanks him."

"You said you believed Mrs. Whitaker poisoned her husband," I reminded her.

"She could have. But you are right, Mr. Herbert could have done it, well enough. He was here last night, before they all left for the dinner, and didn't they have a row? We could hear it downstairs in my kitchen, the two of them standing on the doorstep next door, yelling like stevedores. At least, Mr. Herbert was shouting. Mr. Whitaker never raises his voice."

"I wonder what they could have been arguing about." I put on a tone of mild curiosity in attempt to disguise my blatant hint.

Mrs. Cullen didn't need much of a push. "I can tell you exactly. Mr. Herbert had made a very foolish investment with an unscrupulous gentleman and now owes this gentleman quite a lot of money."

If Mr. Herbert stood to inherit Mr. Whitaker's wealth, this would give him a strong motivation to rid himself of his uncle. Herbert could pay off the unscrupulous gentleman and then wallow in his uncle's money until he squandered the lot.

I wondered what would happen to Mrs. Whitaker when

Herbert inherited. Would he feel an obligation to look after his aunt? Or would he abandon her?

Had Mr. Whitaker provided for his wife in his will? Or had Mrs. Whitaker's family set up a dower that would keep her well for the rest of her life?

Things I would have to discover. If Mrs. Whitaker became fully dependent on her nephew, who was a spendthrift, she'd be less likely to want to polish off her husband.

However, not all murders were about money, I'd come to discover. Some were caused by intense hatred, some by fear, some by desperation.

I supposed that Mrs. Whitaker might bear great anger at her husband for not giving her children, professing disinterest in offspring to hide the fact. Or perhaps she would do anything to get out of a marriage that was binding her. It was difficult for a woman to be granted a divorce or even an annulment without very obvious cause, or without the support of a prominent family behind her.

"Goodness, we're at Hanover Square already," Mrs. Cullen announced.

We had emerged onto the wide square with a garden in its midst. Fine homes marched along on either side of us, but commercial interests, in the form of a bank, had intruded on one end.

Not far from that was the Oriental Club, where gentlemen who'd been in India and other parts of the Eastern world could gather with their mates and have a chinwag about all they'd seen. Mr. Davis had told me that the Duke of Wellington, that hero who'd tossed Napoleon out of Spain and then trounced him at Waterloo, had been its president long ago.

I briefly wondered if the gentlemen of the club insisted on Indian cuisine to remind them of their travels, and if so, whether their chef would share recipes. Mrs. Bywater would never hold with me putting curried dishes on the table, but I might like to try some for myself.

We strolled through the square and continued to Oxford Street, where an overfull omnibus rumbled toward us.

"We've had such an interesting chat that I hate to leave you," Mrs. Cullen said. "Perhaps the omnibus can take you to a market?" She asked the question hopefully.

"My usual is the other direction, Mrs. Cullen. So happy to have met you today."

"Indeed, Mrs. Holloway." She quickened her pace as the omnibus rolled to a stop, disgorging passengers. "Perhaps you can return for a cup of tea on your day out. I would welcome the company."

"Perhaps," I said, promising nothing. "Good afternoon, Mrs. Cullen."

"Afternoon, Mrs. Holloway." Mrs. Cullen trotted to the omnibus, admonishing the driver to wait for her. I heard her voice raised to someone inside, telling him he was a perfectly fit young man and could give up his seat to a lady who was obviously huffing and puffing.

The omnibus lumbered into traffic, Mrs. Cullen's stentorian strains fading. I turned my feet the other way, heading down Oxford Street toward the greengrocer I did not really need to visit.

I purchased some fresh herbs there, having to pick through them before I found some that were not too wilted. One must shop for produce early in the morning, because all the best bits are gone before noon.

I could not reasonably extend my errand any longer, so I returned home after this.

Tess had continued with supper preparations in my absence. I divested myself of my coat and the herbs and joined her to finish the meal.

Supper went up and was consumed in its entirety. No one fell ill tonight, and Mrs. Bywater did not come down to accuse me of serving tainted food. I noted that her worries on that account had not prevented her from eating heartily this evening.

Tess and I finished feeding the staff then prepared for breakfast in the morning, as usual. Once Tess and the other servants had gone to bed, I sat alone at my table, the rest of the house asleep, making notes about today's meals in my little book.

A muffled tap on the outside door made me drop my pencil. I hurried to unlock it, knowing who stood on the other side. Daniel had begun to knock in a certain pattern when he visited at night, so I'd know it was he and not a burglar or other criminal trying to gain entry. I did tell him that someone bent on committing a crime would hardly knock, but he insisted.

I opened the door, not minding at all when Daniel took a step inside, cupped my face in his gloved hands, and kissed me.

He melted me, did Daniel McAdam. I wanted to stand so with him the rest of the night, but the December wind pouring down the stairs was raw. I pulled him inside and bolted the door.

"It's too cold for you to be wandering about outdoors." I hastened to the tea kettle and poured more hot water into the pot, setting out another cup. "Come and warm yourself."

"My intent exactly, Kat." Daniel peeled off his coat and gloves, hanging them up with his hat, then took a stool at the table.

While the tea steeped, I found some tea cakes and another wedge of plum tart, setting all in front of him.

"Did you come with news?" I asked as I poured the tea. "Or is this a social visit?"

"Both." Daniel curved his hands around the mug I slid to him and took a grateful sip of the hot brew. "As ever, I come to gaze upon you and listen to your voice, even when you explain to me what a fool I am. But I also came to tell you about Mr. Whitaker's supposed ladybird."

"Did you?" The small dart of uneasiness that touched me surprised me. I wondered if Daniel had visited the young lady in his guise of vacant upper-class gentleman or the suave City gent. Either way, I did not like the idea of him sitting alone with a seductress.

"Yes." Daniel took another sip of tea, oblivious of my apprehension. "She is not, in fact, his mistress. She is, instead, his daughter."

CHAPTER 3

I stared at Daniel, dumbfounded, my teacup halfway to my lips. Of all the things I expected him to tell me, it was not this.

"But Mrs. Cullen said he was … incapable."

"Who is Mrs. Cullen?" Daniel asked in perplexity.

"The cook to the Whitakers' next-door neighbor. She told me Mr. Whitaker could not sire children."

Daniel's brows rose. "You learned much quickly." He turned to his tea cakes, breaking one apart. "It is true that Whitaker and his wife have never had children. The lady, Miss McCafferty, is the offspring of an early dalliance, before Whitaker met his wife."

I pushed aside my surprise to think this through. "She cannot be a young woman." The Whitakers, if I were to judge from what little I'd glimpsed of them, were in their late fifties or early sixties.

"She is thirty-two. The Whitakers have been married for thirty years."

"Then it must be Mrs. Whitaker who cannot have children," I concluded. Pity touched me.

Daniel shrugged. "Perhaps Whitaker suffered from some illness or accident between his dalliance and his marriage.

According to Miss McCafferty, she learned only a few years ago that her father was alive. Whitaker heard her mother had died, and that she'd borne a child at the relevant time. Whitaker had a private inquiry agent locate her, and also determine that she was indeed his daughter. He's been visiting her since then, giving her funds and getting to know her. Miss McCafferty says Mr. Whitaker is a pleasant gentleman, and she is happy he found her. She is an agreeable young woman herself."

I was back to my twinge of disquiet, which I did not understand. "I am pleased you found her so," I said, a bit stiffly.

Daniel's brows creased. "I never spoke to the lady."

"Oh." I gazed at him in confusion. "Then how do you know all this?"

"I sent Errol to call on her." Daniel grinned. "Mr. Fielding, the humble vicar, petitioning for one of his many charities. He ingratiated himself into Miss McCafferty's sitting room, and she told him everything."

"Oh." The syllable escaped my mouth again.

It made perfect sense that Daniel would bid Mr. Fielding, his scoundrel foster brother, to undertake the task. Mr. Fielding truly was a vicar—he had a living in Shadwell and had recently been made an assistant bishop to his parish. A vicar would seem harmless and be welcomed in to chat with the lady of the house.

"Are you well, Kat?" Daniel peered at me in puzzlement.

"Of course. I didn't understand that Mr. Fielding had obtained the information, not you. That is all."

Daniel studied me a while longer, then his face cleared, and his eyes began to twinkle. "Kat Holloway, were you afraid I would succumb to the lady's charms?"

I straightened my spine, indignant. "Of course not."

"I'd be pleased if you were." Daniel shoved aside his tea and reached across the table to clasp my hands. "Tell me you were worried I'd look elsewhere, my Kat. It would mean you care where my yearnings lay."

I slid free of his grip. "Do not be ridiculous. If you had visited with Miss McCafferty, it would only be to ascertain whether she had a motive to murder Mr. Whitaker. Nothing more. I know this."

"I prefer your worry. A worry quite unfounded, I will add." Daniel reached for my hands again, this time not letting me pull away. "I have eyes for no other lady than your good self, my dear Kat. That is the truth, and that will never change."

My voice softened, in spite of myself. "How can you say never? You do not know how long we will be friends, or when our lives will take us apart. None of us can tell what the future will bring."

So many things could happen to Daniel as he drove about the city or hunted sinister criminals for Mr. Monaghan. So might they happen to Grace, or James, or Joanna and Sam and their family. We never knew how long we had with anyone.

I ended up clinging to Daniel's hands, and his amusement changed to concern.

"We take it one day at a time, my love," he said in soothing tones. "Treasure what we have while we have it."

"I do treasure it." I met his gaze, my eyes stinging. "Each and every time I am with you."

Daniel rose and came to me without releasing me. He lifted me from the chair and slid his arms around me. "What you say now pleases me even more."

The kitchen went quiet as we created another moment to cherish in lonely nights to come.

Daniel's kisses always left me breathless. When he finally eased from me, brushing my lips with his thumb, I had to sit down rather suddenly.

"Eat your tart," I said, the words faint. "I must rid myself of all these blasted plums."

Daniel's laughter rang out. The lower floor was empty, so I did not worry about anyone overhearing.

"The trials and tribulations of a put-upon cook." Daniel

continued to chuckle as he resumed his seat and lifted his fork. "Do tell me what you discovered from the Whitaker's neighbor's cook."

My voice grew strong again as I recounted Mrs. Cullen's tale, checking the notes I'd made tonight to be certain I told him all.

"Hmm," Daniel said when I finished. "We have a nephew who needs his uncle's funds, a wife who apparently dotes on her husband, and a daughter happy she's found her father. The nephew is the most likely candidate, but would he have a chance to slip something into his uncle's sherry without being noticed?"

"There is also the man who owes Mr. Whitaker money. Cynthia mentioned him—what was his name?" I consulted my notes. "Hardy, that was it. We must find out about Mr. Hardy."

"Again, this man needs to have had the opportunity to give Mr. Whitaker poison. The wife is still the most likely person, or one of Whitaker's servants. If any are unhappy with their lot and blame the master, it would be easy for one of them to slip a dollop into his soup."

"If every disgruntled servant doctored their master's soup or tea or sherry, there would be an amazing number of deaths in Mayfair," I said.

Daniel laughed again. "I take your point. Also, servants are usually the first to be accused. Mrs. Bywater was very quick to point at you."

"She was indeed." I shivered. "She would be happier if she could find a good reason to dismiss me. I'd give noticed and seek another house to work in, but I stay because of Lady Cynthia and Tess. They'd be unhappy if I left."

"A good many people would be." Daniel swallowed another bite of tart. "They need you, Kat. Mrs. Bywater needs you as well, though she doesn't understand that. From what I have observed, she is a lady who wants very much to be in charge of everything. When she comes across a person she cannot control absolutely—

you, for instance, and Lady Cynthia—she compensates for this by finding fault wherever she can."

This described Mrs. Bywater exactly. Should I pity her, rather than grow irritated with her? A difficult thing to do.

I turned to a clean page in my notebook. "What next? I suppose we must discover whether Miss McCafferty benefits if Mr. Whitaker dies. If he visits her regularly, she herself could feed him a slow poison. Or perhaps Mr. Whitaker meets this Mr. Hardy who owes him money at their club, and Mr. Hardy puts something into his brandy or whiskey, or whatever Mr. Whitaker consumes there."

"I will send Errol back to Miss McCafferty to find out more." Daniel finished off the tart and pushed away his plate. "Thanos is looking into what poisons produce the symptoms Mr. Whitaker exhibits. Tomorrow is your day out. Would you find a moment to stop by Mr. Thanos's flat and hear his report?"

"Won't he be at the Polytechnic?" I asked in surprise.

"Not tomorrow morning." Daniel rose, and I hopped to my feet. "He would enjoy living at the Poly, but Lady Cynthia and I have convinced him to spend a few mornings at home resting and reading, to prepare for his lectures the rest of the week."

"Of course," I said. "I cannot stay long, though."

"No, indeed, and I will not ask you to. I have an idea—you stop at Thanos's flat, and then I will accompany you to the Millburns'. There is a pantomime at the Savoy Theatre tomorrow afternoon. Do you think Grace would enjoy it?"

I brightened. "I believe she would." I had not seen a panto in a very long time, myself. "I would as well," I said with enthusiasm.

Daniel chuckled. "I will try not to be aggrieved that you grow more animated about viewing a stage performance than you do about seeing *me*."

My brows rose. "Well, it's a rare thing for me to attend such entertainment, whereas I speak with you frequently." A smile accompanied my words, so he'd know I was teasing.

Daniel studied me as though he wasn't certain, but he drew near and kissed my lips. "I look forward to it, Mrs. Holloway."

Before leaving in the morning, I helped Tess with breakfast and made more notes on my plans for Christmas dinner.

Mrs. Bywater had given me a list of all she wanted, which was overlong and ridiculous for their gathering of six people. Possibly eight or ten, Mrs. Redfern, the housekeeper, had mentioned to me, tight-lipped, yesterday evening, which annoyed me. Adding last-minute guests meant each person would have to take smaller helpings. If I made too much food to compensate for possible extra servings, I'd be berated for wasting it.

Soup would figure largely into this menu, I'd decided. Cynthia's father had promised game from his estate, which could be put into a stew. Not trusting the earl entirely, I planned a julienne of vegetables soup and a thick carrot one as well. Several fish dishes would finish off the first course.

Mrs. Bywater insisted on a whole roast goose, and the best vendor for fowl in Covent Garden promised me one. In case he could not provide it for some reason, I would include a fricassee of chicken and leg of mutton.

Plenty of tarts, breads, and cakes would follow, including the pièce de résistance, the Christmas pudding. This would be served with brandy poured over it and flamed, with hard sauce on the side.

"Hard sauce?" Tess asked me this morning. "Why would someone want sauce that's hard? Do you need a chisel to eat it?" She chortled at the notion.

"It is a misnomer," I assured her as I arranged egg cups and piles of buttered toast on the platter to send upstairs. "Probably because of all the butter in it. It's a mixture of that, icing sugar, and brandy. You spoon it onto the hot pudding, and it melts over it. It's quite delicious."

"I should think it would be." Tess smacked her lips. "We'll have to taste a large portion, to make certain all is well."

"Of course, Tess." I ought to admonish her for wanting to help herself to the Bywaters' food, but I was in a good humor this morning. I always was, on Thursdays.

As soon as breakfast went up in the dumbwaiter, I pulled off my apron, changed to my second-best frock, and took up my coat. Tess waved me out, and I climbed the stairs to the street, breathing in the frigid air in release.

I had already sent a note to Joanna saying I'd be a tad late for my visit with Grace, and I turned my steps toward Regent Street. My path would take me along Brook Street to Hanover Square, as it had yesterday. Today, however, I heard soft footfalls behind me, ones that hurried when I did, slowed when I slowed. They stopped altogether when I halted, pretending to check for something in my handbag.

A lesser woman might have been frightened. I only quickened my pace, forcing my follower to keep up, and turned into Brook Street.

I gazed curiously at the Whitaker's home as I passed it. Curtains were drawn over most of the windows, but no black wreath had been hung on the door, to my relief. There was illness in the house, the facade told me, but not death.

As I hastened past the house where Mrs. Cullen worked, hoping she would not emerge to engage me in long conversation, a plain black carriage halted at the Whitakers' doorway.

A man in a dark coat and tall hat descended, a large valise clutched in his hand. From his dress and nondescript carriage, I guessed he was the doctor. Dr. Burnley, Cynthia had said his name was.

The door opened before Dr. Burnley could rap upon it. A

footman let him inside, but calmly, without agitation. This must be a routine visit, not an urgent summons.

I slowed my steps to watch, but there was little more to see. The footman shut the door and the carriage creaked away, the coachman heading to the mews to tend the horses until the doctor was ready to leave.

"I know you are there, James," I said to the air. "Come out here where I can speak to you."

A moment later, a tall lad materialized from the shadows of a stairwell across the street, beaming at me. "Sorry, Mrs. H.," he said as he jogged to me. "Dad told me to keep an eye on you. You don't always take care, he says."

CHAPTER 4

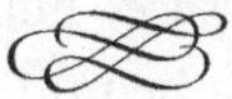

James admitted this to me without shame, his warm smile so like his father's.

"I take plenty of care," I said impatiently. "I am off to meet him and Mr. Thanos, in any case, not walking about alone in Seven Dials." I forced my annoyance to recede. "It is fortunate you are here, no matter what the reason. Will you go to Brooks's Mews and strike up a conversation with the driver of the doctor's coach? It's the one that stopped here a moment ago."

"Aye, the doctor comes and goes a good deal at this house. Poor gent is very ill, ain't he?"

I ought to have known James had already grasped what was going on. I also liked his compassion.

"He is indeed," I said. "I have no excuse for chatting with the doctor, but maybe his coachman will gossip. Right now, information is what I need, and I believe I can walk all the way to Regent Street without you watching over me."

James nodded readily. "I'll have a chat with the coachman, never you worry. Also, the other grooms and coachmen there. They always know much about the families they work for."

Probably more than the family knew themselves. The Bywaters' coachman, Henry, enjoyed talking about the family to all and sundry. Particularly to me when he had reason to come into the kitchen or when I took food to the coach house. Henry had concluded he had no chance to woo me, but that did not stop him from trying to buttonhole me every time I came nigh him.

"Don't tell Dad," James added in sudden trepidation.

"It will be our secret," I assured him.

James saluted me and dashed off, his long legs carrying him around the corner in a flash. I continued on toward Hanover Square and emerged into Regent Street a few steps from the fine building that housed Mr. Thanos's rooms. He'd been provided them by the Polytechnic, which was not far up the road in Cavendish Square.

The landlady of this building knew me from my previous visits. She bade me a cordial good morning as I climbed the wide staircase to Mr. Thanos's floor.

The house, built more than sixty years ago, had grand columns and high ceilings, black-and-white tiled floors, and polished marble banisters. I skimmed my fingers along the railing, liking the smooth feeling of the stone, and arrived at a tall black door on an upper floor.

It opened as I approached, Daniel framed in the opening. Behind him, Mr. Thanos was rising, and Cynthia, in a man's coat, came forward to greet me.

Friends were wonderful things, I decided as I settled into an armchair before Mr. Thanos's fire. Cynthia insisted on pouring the tea the landlady had brought, and she spilled only a little.

"The doctor is calling on Mr. Whitaker as we speak," I said, and recounted how I'd seen him. I omitted that I'd asked James to follow his coachman. Daniel did not need to know his ploy to have me watched had not worked—I didn't want him admonishing the boy.

"I have heard of Dr. Burnley." Mr. Thanos took the teacup Cynthia handed him and sloshed even more into the saucer as she smiled at him. "A chappie I know at the Polytechnic knows him, or knows of him. Says he's quite good. His patients generally get well, apart from Mr. Whitaker, that is. But some illnesses can't be healed, sadly."

That was true. Certain maladies could send a person into a long decline, from which there was no recovery. I was always grateful for my own robust constitution.

"Mr. Whitaker's symptoms are natural, then?" I asked.

I both hoped so and didn't. If Mr. Whitaker was truly ill, then my reputation was clear, but I did not wish a serious illness on anyone. On the other hand, if poison was the culprit, an antidote might be found to help him.

"I have been reading up," Mr. Thanos said. "Medicine is not my forte, except for electrical impulses of the brain and nerves, which are most fascinating. His symptoms Cyn—erm, Lady Cynthia—tells me her friend said are tiredness, a rapid heartbeat even when he's resting, an inability to catch his breath, and pain when he needs to, erm, relieve himself."

Mr. Thanos's smooth face went very red, but I jotted this down in the notebook I'd slid into my handbag before I'd left the kitchen.

"Are these the same symptoms arsenic causes?" I asked him.

"No." Mr. Thanos said the word sharply then looked apologetic.

I couldn't blame him for snapping. At one time he had been the victim of arsenical poisoning, and he'd become quite ill. We'd feared he would not recover, but with Daniel and me nursing him, he'd come through.

"No," Mr. Thanos repeated in a softer tone. "From what Lady Cynthia's friend described, it is not arsenic. He does not have abdominal pain or jaundice."

"He did heave up your dinner," Cynthia informed me. "Hence why Auntie feared he'd eaten something untoward in our dining room. Don't worry, Mrs. H. I won't let her sack you for it as she threatens. The rest of us would have had our heads over basins if something had been in the food."

"Very true," Mr. Thanos agreed brightly.

"Conclusions," Daniel broke in. "Either Mr. Whitaker simply has an ongoing illness, or someone managed to give him a dose that no one else received."

I had listed all the possible ways Mr. Whitaker could have ingested poison, and now I read them out. "In his tea, sherry, whiskey, or other beverage before he arrived for dinner, suggesting a poison that acts within an hour or so. If someone wishes him to linger for a certain amount of time—weeks, perhaps—they could slip it into whatever he drinks before bed each night, or in any other draughts his doctor prescribes him. Some poisons can be rubbed into the skin, perhaps in a salve. Monkshood, for instance."

"You do have a gruesome knowledge of noxious substances," Daniel observed, his forehead creasing.

"A cook must always be careful," I answered. "There are many things lying about households that might make their way into food if one is not watchful. Arsenic is used in dyes and also to keep away rodents, as is strychnine. Ergot of rye is a fungus that clings to rye and wheat and could get into the flour. It can be deadly. You usually deliver flour to me, Daniel."

He blenched. "From a reputable source, I assure you. They make certain all they sell is pure."

"Ergot of rye produces symptoms similar to Mr. Whitaker's," I continued. "Then there is ipecac, which is commonly given as a purge but is fatal in high doses. Tansy tea, which can also be a medicine, is present in many households, as is pennyroyal oil. Not to mention all the poisonous plants in the garden."

"Damnation," Cynthia said with fervor. "Makes me not want to eat another bite."

"Mrs. Holloway's cooking is always good," Mr. Thanos said.

"And safe." He wasn't being kind—he believed it. I sent him a smile.

"So, you see," I went on, "the poison could have come from anywhere, even accidentally. If their cook had been careless, others would be ill, as Lady Cynthia has pointed out. Have any in their household been, do you know, Lady Cynthia?"

"My friend who shares the doctor with the Whitakers says not. Judith also had a chat with Mrs. Whitaker, who is an acquaintance of Judith's mum. Mrs. Whitaker insists the only person in the house who is ill is her husband. None of the servants show any symptoms, and the nephew, who visits often, is right as rain. The old army friend, Mr. Hardy, who can't pay Mr. Whitaker what he owes him, is another frequent visitor to the house. He is as vigorous as ever." Cynthia poured droplets of tea from her saucer into her cup and took a sip. "Judith wonders if Mr. Hardy is looking to get his feet under Mrs. Whitaker's table. Sounds as though he's interested enough in her."

"That is a possibility," I conceded. "Suppose Mr. Hardy comes to visit as often as he can in the guise of a friend and taints Mr. Whitaker's whiskey. If he and Mr. Whitaker meet at their club, Mr. Hardy would have opportunity there as well."

"Hardy and Whitaker belong to the Oriental Club, as both did business in India some time ago," Cynthia said. "They went out in the army and then stayed for a bit. It's one reason Whitaker is so rich. Young Herbert wouldn't be admitted to the club, except as a guest of his uncle, and not regularly. Herbert likely only visits Whitaker at the house in Brook Street."

I sighed, discouraged. "Any of them could be hastening Mr. Whitaker to his grave." I closed the notebook, but my voice hardened. "We cannot let them."

Daniel's affable persona fell away, and the grim man who chased criminals for the police appeared. "No, we won't."

This had gone beyond me proving I'd not served a contaminated meal and saving my job. Mr. Whitaker was a wealthy man, and several people stood to gain from his death. The nephew and the insolvent friend would benefit, and perhaps the daughter would too, if Mr. Whitaker had put her into his will. She might have decided she'd suffered from her illegitimacy long enough, and she'd had opportunity to doctor his tea.

I thought of the poor man suffering in his bed, and I determined to stop it. Daniel met my gaze, understanding. Cynthia and Mr. Thanos looked adamant as well. Between the four of us, I decided, the killer didn't stand a chance.

DANIEL ESCORTED ME FROM THE SOBERING MEETING AT MR. Thanos's flat and the rest of the way to the Millburns'. We tramped down Oxford Street and over the Holborn Viaduct to Newgate Street in silence, making our way to Cheapside. From there we took a small turning called Clover Lane and arrived at the house where my daughter lived.

Grace greeted me with her usual loving exuberance, and I sank into her embrace. My girl was getting so tall, I realized as I pulled away to look at her. She was my height now and possibly would grow even more.

I'd have to decide soon what was to become of her. I did not want her in service, as I had been, but there were not many choices for the daughter of a domestic.

I pressed aside such worries to think about later. Grace was pleased to see Daniel and excited about our treat out today.

Daniel took us to the Savoy Theatre just off the Strand, a fairly new place of entertainment, lavish and shining. Though I protested I could pay our way, Daniel wouldn't hear of it. He procured the tickets and ushered us inside, and I decided, for Grace's sake, to cease my fussing.

James slid into the seat beside Daniel as the first play started.

He gave me a surreptitious nod then greeted his father and Grace with his customary cheerfulness.

Several pantos would run today. The first was *Puss in Boots,* a favorite, with plenty of songs, antics, and actors in amusing animal costumes. The lady in the breeches part was quite comely, with her long legs displayed in white tights. I would never have the courage to wear such attire, but she was so lively and funny as the hero with his magical cat, that I soon forgot about these concerns and settled in to enjoy the play.

Grace bounced in her seat, most unlike her, loudly shouting the responses to the actors. I found my voice hoarse as I yelled along with her, collapsing into laughter with my daughter.

Daniel also bellowed with enthusiasm. James was a master at it, his words booming over the crowd's. His voice had grown deep, James swiftly becoming a man.

Daniel squeezed my hand at one point, his broad smile warming me through.

This is happiness, the words came to me. My resentment about my plight in life, my envy of those who had true homes to go to at Christmas, began to dissolve.

I had a beautiful daughter, dear friends, and a man with whom I could be wholly myself. Daniel not only admired me, but he put up with my insatiable curiosity, my quick temper, and my absolute need to put Grace first. Daniel had a good heart, and I knew I was lucky I had him in my life.

As I watched *Puss* and the following even more elaborate production of *Aladdin,* a sort of peace settled over me. These moments, stolen when I could take them, were joy. I would not trade them for all the riches in the world.

I clung to that feeling as we walked home, James darting off once we reached Cheapside.

Joanna invited Daniel to stay once we reached her house. I thought he'd beg off, saying he had much to do, but he accepted, and we sat in the parlor, sipping tea and enjoying conversation. Grace lingered with me instead of running back to her studies or to play with Joanna's oldest daughter who'd become her closest friend.

Joanna's husband, Sam, arrived home as the windows grew dark, and he joined us for tea and chatter. He and Daniel got along well, I observed, as the two men exchanged banter and laughter.

When I had to depart, bitterness stirred in my heart again. Joanna could remain in this warm house with her husband and children, whereas I had to return to drudgery before I went to sleep in my cold attic room alone.

Daniel, bless him, offered to see me home.

Once I tore myself from Grace, Daniel hailed a hansom, and we huddled together under the lap robe in the frigid December air.

"What is it, Kat?" Daniel asked, sensing my mood.

"Oh, I am merely being disgruntled." I stretched my tired feet under the blanket. "Sometimes I wish I could chuck it all and run far away—with Grace, of course. Instead, I must argue with a woman who will have the perfect Christmas dinner, even though she has no knowledge about food and how it is prepared. If she is not ecstatically pleased with the Christmas meal, it will be all my fault, in her opinion."

"Why don't you then?" Daniel asked.

"Why don't I what?"

"Chuck it all. Hand Mrs. Bywater your apron and tell her she must find another cook to put up with her. Go to a village in the country and set up the tea shop you dream of."

I stared at him as he ran through this scenario, his teasing tone vanishing.

His sudden seriousness shook me from my doldrums, and my common sense returned. "Because, my dear Daniel, shoes and frocks for a girl who grows out of them each year cost money. So does food to eat and a roof to sleep under. I did not have the fortune to be born with coffers full of cash, you know."

"I wish you did not always have to be worried about money," Daniel said, almost fiercely.

"We all do, even gentlemen who sit in exclusive clubs." I thought of Mr. Hardy and how desperate he might feel, owing Mr. Whitaker a large debt. "I will ask you in return, why do you not tell Mr. Monaghan to go hang and depart London with James for this picturesque village in the country? Whose inhabitants likely would not welcome strangers from London without some sort of introduction. We could be anybody."

Daniel listened with a scowl that lightened as I ran through my speech. The softness reentered his voice as I finished.

"As always, Kat, you have more sense than any person I've ever known. You know good and well why I can't tell Monaghan to go hang, as much as I'd like to. I want James to have a father who is not rotting in prison."

"Mr. Monaghan would not dare," I said with indignation.

"Indeed, he would. Even the hardest inspectors at the Yard are afraid of Monaghan. He is ruthless." Daniel's smile returned, and he kissed my cheek. "I will cling to the fact that when you spoke of retiring to our imaginary village, you implied that we'd go there together."

I started. "Did I?"

"You did. I will also enjoy that you said it spontaneously, without thought." Daniel brushed back a lock of my hair, which had straggled from beneath my hat when he'd kissed me. "I will think on this for the rest of the day and let it warm me in the winter's darkness."

For my part, I would remember his lips on my cheek, his touch on my hair, and his laughter as we'd enjoyed the panto.

"Leave off," I said softly. "Daft man."

JAMES WAS WAITING AT THE RAILINGS THAT EVENING AFTER SUPPER when I took scraps outside to the unfortunates.

"Doctor's coachman was friendly enough," he reported when I finished and turned to him. "Dr. Burnley's a personable man, coachman says. Doesn't mind a gab with his servants."

"A good thing for us," I observed.

James leaned negligently against the railings, his stance so like his father's that my heart squeezed.

"Coachman says he's a good doctor too," James continued. "Wants to heal his patients, not just collect his fee. He's been tending the Whitaker family for ages. He's worried about Mr. Whitaker's health, thinking the man's about to die."

"Oh, dear. I am sorry to hear it."

I truly was. It was Christmas, and Mrs. Whitaker didn't need a tragedy just now. Losing a loved one was bad at any time, but in this season, it was doubly hard.

"The doctor's starting to believe Mrs. Whitaker's theory of poison," James went on. "And trying to decide how to cure him."

"Does he suspect what substance it is?" I asked with hope. If that was found, perhaps it could be counteracted.

"Coachman don't know. He's only repeating what he's heard the doc mention in passing."

"Of course." I hid my disappointment.

It would be useful if I could sit Dr. Burnley down and ask him pointed questions, but I would have to invent some excuse to do so. He was not the Bywaters' doctor and so would not call at the Mount Street house.

Not that a doctor visited often. When one of the staff fell sick, Mrs. Bywater dosed them with such foul-tasting remedies they recovered swiftly in order to get away from them. She didn't believe in paying a doctor to attend servants, in any case.

"Coachman did hear the doctor quarreling with Mr. Whitaker lately," James added. "A few weeks ago, that is. At the moment, the poor man can barely speak."

"Oh? Does the coachman know what about?"

"No. Only heard him through the open door. Doc said something like, 'you must put it right,' or 'you must do right by it.' He's not certain. It was only the one time, though. After that, they seemed to be friends again."

It could mean nothing, or be the key to everything. So frustrating not to know.

"Tell your father what you've learned," I said to James. "It might be important." I hesitated. "Perhaps you don't have to mention that I asked you to talk to the coachman instead of following me about."

James's smile grew broader. "I can turn Dad up sweet, don't you worry."

"You don't need to turn him up sweet, James, dear. You ought to obey him when he gives you orders. He has your best interests at heart. Mine too, I suppose."

His brown eyes sparkled with good humor. "Right you are, Mrs. H."

I knew I was inconsistent with my advice to him, but Daniel always left me flummoxed.

"Run home and keep warm," I bade him. "I will have plenty of leftover Christmas pudding in a few days. I'll save some for you to feast on."

James burst out laughing, a joyous sound. The beggars who'd remained to consume the food I'd given them brightened.

"I look forward to that, Mrs. H. A happy Christmas to you."

"Happy Christmas, James." I warmed as he bounded away, waving as he went. Daniel was blessed to have such a son, and I was blessed by him too.

"Mrs. Whitaker would like it if you called on her, Mrs. H.," Cynthia startled me the next morning by saying.

She'd breezed downstairs after breakfast, dressed in a frock with easy lines, the sort she'd begun wearing in the last year or so. She was off to the Polytechnic to help Mr. Thanos and had stopped off in the kitchen on her way out.

"If I called on her?" I asked, mystified. "Why?"

"To help heal her husband," Cynthia said, as though this were a perfectly reasonable explanation. "I said that you'd be able to."

CHAPTER 5

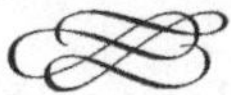

"You told her I would cure her husband?" I burst out. "Have you run mad?" I checked my amazement as I remembered to whom I spoke. "I beg your pardon, Lady Cynthia, but you have confounded me."

Cynthia waved my apology aside. "I am telling it wrong. Judith says I always speak before I have my thoughts in order. I let on to my friend—the one whose mum also has Dr. Burnley for her physician—that you created dishes that made those feeling poorly ever so much better. She told Mrs. Whitaker, who said she'd welcome you to come and give her cook a few of your recipes. Mrs. Whitaker is desperate for her husband to get well."

Her explanation made more sense, but it was still alarming. "You ought to have promised no such thing."

While my broths and blancmanges were likely the reason ailing staff recovered, in spite of Mrs. Bywater's patent medicines, I could not guarantee to cure a bad illness or a poisoning.

"Nonsense. Your cooking will do him a world of good," Cynthia said resolutely. "And it would get you into the house, where you can do some sleuthing. I'll go with you, if you'd like."

Cynthia whirled, ready to rush to the Whitaker house on the moment, but I forestalled her.

"Better that I go on my own," I said quickly. "Besides, Mr. Thanos is counting on you."

Cynthia came to a stop, her skirt swinging. "That is a point. I say, I am sorry, Mrs. H. I thought you'd welcome an entrée into the lion's den."

"I do welcome it." I softened. "I had been looking for a way in. You startled me, is all. I can at least ease the man's suffering a little and perhaps his wife's anxiousness too."

"Excellent. Well, I'm off." Cynthia managed to sneak a scone off a plate before she strode out the door.

Today was Friday, and I had no business leaving the kitchen, but I would have to contrive some excuse. My next afternoon out was not until Monday, which this year was also Christmas Day.

Mrs. Bywater had hinted I should stay home to ensure that Christmas dinner went off without trouble, but I had stood firm. If I gave way in this one instance, Mrs. Bywater would try her best to deprive me of more days out. One must stick to one's principles. Besides, I'd be mad to give up the chance to spend Christmas afternoon with Grace.

I went through the recipes I'd created to aid with digestion and wrote out a few neatly in my notebook. The Whitakers' cook might not be able to read, which meant I'd have to tell her the recipes, or demonstrate them. Many cooks couldn't read at all but had prodigious memories for ingredients and their measurements. But if she could read, I'd leave the pages with her.

Mrs. Bywater found my excuse for me. She didn't come to the kitchen herself, but sent Mrs. Redfern down after luncheon with a message for me.

"The mistress received a note from Mrs. Whitaker." Mrs. Redfern was a haughty woman but shared my impatience with Mrs. Bywater, who had clearly not been raised to deal with a household of servants. "Lady Cynthia sang your praises, and Mrs. Whitaker asked if you could be spared for a few hours."

"Yes, Lady Cynthia mentioned it," I said quickly.

Tess hid a snort as she sauteed chops at the stove. She'd heard my conversation with Cynthia, and she found my ingenuousness amusing.

"Mrs. Whitaker has a bee in her bonnet about her husband being poisoned," Mrs. Redfern said. "The mistress did not say that, but it is obvious she believes it."

At least Mrs. Bywater wasn't continuing to declare that a noxious substance had come from my kitchen. Dare I hope she'd forgotten the matter and ceased blaming me? The lady could so often do an about-turn in her notions, much to our exasperation.

"I will go to Brook Street straightaway." I untied my apron and took up my basket, where I'd already set the recipes as well as a few fresh herbs the Whitakers' cook might not have. "I will return as soon as I am able."

"Before the master is home, anyway," Mrs. Redfern said. "He is weary of Mr. Whitaker, he says. I heard Mr. Bywater remark that the man has been ailing for years but probably will outlive us all."

It was true that some frail people managed to hang on while those who seemed hardy could pop off at a moment's notice.

I kept this observation to myself, donned coat and hat, and left for Brook Street.

Today I did not hesitate when I reached the stairs that led to the Whitakers' kitchen but climbed down them at a swift pace. I rapped on the door at the bottom, which was opened by a red-faced and sweating young woman.

"What yer want?" she asked in breathless apprehension.

A stronger voice boomed behind her. "Who is it, Agnes?"

"I dunno, Mrs. Provost. Some woman."

"Oh, for heaven's sake." Footsteps sounded, and an older woman with iron-gray hair under a cook's cap glared around Agnes at me. "Well? Who are you?"

I met the woman's gaze without flinching. "I am Mrs. Holloway, Lady Cynthia Shires's cook. Mrs. Whitaker wished me to bring you some recipes."

"Oh." Mrs. Provost looked me up and down, obviously not pleased with what she saw. "So she told me. Well, you'd better come in."

Not the most gracious welcome, but I slid inside and shrugged off my coat, hanging it up along with my hat. Mrs. Provost watched me sourly as I approached the kitchen table, which was strewn with vegetables and greens. All looked fresh and of good quality, which was a relief.

"You're young for a cook," Mrs. Provost said as I set my basket on a chair and removed the sheaf of recipes.

"I trained thoroughly and advanced quickly." I was proud of how I'd risen from cook's assistant to head cook at a rapid pace, due to both my skills and excellent instruction. My mother had found talented women to take me under their wing.

"Hmph." Mrs. Provost clearly did not approve. "Well, you'd better show me the recipes. The mistress believes we will magic the master back to health and rid him of her imagined poisons."

"Perhaps not imagined," I said. "Bad substances can enter food without our knowledge."

"Not in this kitchen," Mrs. Provost snapped. "I allowed you down here, Mrs. Holloway, only because Mrs. Cullen next door spoke highly of you."

"That was kind of her," I murmured.

"She's a gossipy busybody." Mrs. Provost took up a chef's knife and brought it down on a clump of unsuspecting parsley resting on the table. Green bits flew everywhere. "I took her at her word, but not to have you come into my kitchen and accuse me of all sorts."

"Not accusing," I said, my tone firm. "But we do not always know what is in our ingredients. Mr. Whitaker has been ill for some time, I hear."

"Yes, but it's nothing to do with me."

Mrs. Provost continued to slice savagely, thrusting aside the parsley to start in on spring onions. Parsley should be chopped at the last minute, not left sitting about to lose its flavor, but I did not remark upon it.

"How long has he been poorly?" I asked.

The assistant, Agnes, answered. "A few years now, missus. Ever since he came back from Cheltenham, where he stayed with his nephew one summer. His friend Mr. Hardy was there too. Mrs. Whitaker thinks he over— over— over-something. Too much walking and riding, she meant. He's been sickly ever since."

Over-exerted himself possibly. If a man was not used to hearty country walks and riding breakneck across meadows, it might strain his already weak constitution.

"Nonsense," Mrs. Provost declared. "He was all right when he came home. But soon after, he started staying out much more than he used to. Spending nights at his club and such things. The doctor suspects he's keeping another woman, and *she* has made him so ill. You know what tarts are like."

The woman in question was not a tart, but his daughter, though it was clear Mrs. Provost did not know that. I supposed the shock of finding the daughter might have weakened Mr. Whitaker, but surely, he'd have recovered of that by now. Of the walking and riding as well. Mrs. Whitaker probably had the right of it.

I showed Mrs. Provost the recipes I'd brought—clear soups, bland custards, and a blancmange flavored with almonds. All slipped down easily and sat lightly on the stomach.

It turned out that Mrs. Provost could indeed read. She peered at my words, her lips moving as she made them out.

"Nothing remarkable in these recipes," she pronounced when

she finished. "I suppose we'd better make them, though, or the mistress will be displeased."

Agnes gathered the ingredients, and we began. Mrs. Provost, for her ill temper, proved to be a competent cook. After an hour or so, we had a repast that should appeal to any invalid.

The house had no dumbwaiter, and the footmen, Mrs. Provost told me, were too proud to run errands for her. Possibly they didn't wish to venture into the kitchen and fall under the lash of Mrs. Provost's tongue.

I volunteered to carry the heavy tray upstairs, and neither Mrs. Provost nor Agnes argued with me. Neither of them helped me, either. They both obviously believed my errand was pointless.

I struggled with the door at the top of the stairs, which was wrenched open for me so suddenly that I nearly dropped the tray.

"Whoops." A tall young man with a shock of light-brown hair in a tailored suit steadied the tray and bathed me in a winsome smile. "Have a care. I heard you scrabbling at the door—lucky I did, isn't it? Who are you? A new maid?"

"I am Mrs. Holloway," I explained. "Your aunt asked me to prepare some dishes for your uncle."

"Ah, yes, the cook who made us such a wonderful meal the other night. I ate until I was stuffed and wished there was more."

"You are too kind," I said, inclining my head.

My guess that he was Mr. Herbert Whitaker, the wastrel nephew and heir, proved correct.

"My aunt dotes on my uncle, she does," Herbert said good-naturedly. "I'll show you to the sickroom, shall I?"

"That would be most welcome."

Herbert didn't relieve me of my burden but scampered up the stairs as though I could follow at his rapid pace. He waited for me with some patience in the hall two flights up and ushered me into a dark bedroom.

The chamber would have been a fine one were it not so gloomy. The curtains were pulled tightly shut, with only one gas lamp to light the winter day. A large bed with a heavily carved head and footboard dominated the room, flanked by matching night tables. Ponderous but comfortable-looking chairs and a chaise had been placed around the large room, with a full bookcase against one wall. Knitted throws waited on each chair so a person could bundle up cozily while he or she read.

Mr. Whitaker was not in the bed but on the chaise, wrapped in blankets, with a square table pulled next to him. On this lay a sheaf of newspapers as well as a pot of tea and a glass of what looked like cordial.

Mr. Whitaker was painfully thin, his chest sunken, his cheeks gray. The whites of his eyes held a yellowish tinge.

"Good afternoon, Uncle," Herbert sang out as he admitted me. "This is Mrs. Holloway. The cook who made such a splendid meal when we visited Mr. Bywater the other night."

Mr. Whitaker sent me a wan smile. "Such a treat. I commend you for the meal, Mrs. Holloway. I was sorry to have taken a turn and not finished it. Did you come to find out why I'd left too much food on my plate?"

His good humor about his weak state was both charming and sad.

"Not at all." I spoke in my best no-nonsense voice. "Mrs. Whitaker asked me to make a few dishes to settle your stomach, and I was happy to oblige."

"You're a cheerful cook." Mr. Whitaker's hands moved on the blanket. "A novelty in this house. Well, Mrs. Holloway, I will attempt a few mouthfuls, but I warn you, my appetite is not what it once was."

"It will do you good, Uncle." Herbert clasped his hands and kept his smile fixed on Mr. Whitaker. "If you eat up and rest as the doctor says, you'll be well in no time."

"You are young and optimistic," Mr. Whitaker answered dryly. "Perhaps it is just as well for you that I am finished. You can come into your legacy and begin to live your life."

"Do not say that," Herbert exclaimed in trepidation. "No reason for me to settle down so soon. I'd rather be touching you for my allowance for years to come."

I concentrated on dishing out a bit of custard garnished with fresh mint during this exchange, pretending not to listen. Herbert sounded genuinely concerned that his uncle might cease to be, rather than a young man eager to inherit a surfeit of wealth.

"It will be the making of you," Mr. Whitaker assured him. "Your aunt will look after you. And you her."

"Please don't speak so, Uncle," Herbert said in distress. "You've been ill like this before and recovered. No reason you shouldn't again."

"The very young believe no one will ever die," Mr. Whitaker said to me as I set the bowl of custard on the table next to him. I'd added plenty of vanilla and a little nutmeg to warm the stomach. "But I've put everything to rights and can leave all in Mrs. Whitaker's capable hands. I have no regrets."

Interesting. Did he mean he'd told his wife about his by-blow daughter? Had he provided for the young woman? Or only for Herbert?

My speculations were interrupted by the arrival of the doctor himself. I'd only seen Dr. Burnley in a greatcoat and hat, and without them he proved to have a slight build and balding head, a graying moustache on his thin face. His brown eyes filled with concern as he took in the scene.

"What is that you're eating?" he exclaimed as Mr. Whitaker finished off his first spoonful. "You must be very careful what you ingest."

"It's only a bit of custard," I said. "It will do him no harm."

"And very good custard, too." Mr. Whitaker spooned up another mouthful. "Much better than those foul concoctions you feed me, Burnley."

Doctor Burnley frowned in displeasure. "If you can keep it down, it might be all right. But you must rest."

"I am tired of resting." Mr. Whitaker ate another mouthful—nothing wrong with his appetite today. "It is wearying, all this resting."

Herbert chuckled. "Very clever, Uncle."

"Speaking of clever, Herbert, you must meet Mr. Hardy at our club for me," Mr. Whitaker instructed.

I listened intently as I stirred the broth and added a bit of chopped parsley to the bowl.

"At the Oriental?" Herbert sounded pained. "Stuffy place full of tedious old men. If one doesn't know anything about the East India Company, one is sneered at."

"Several of those tedious old men paid me compliments on my bright and cheerful nephew last time I took you there," Mr. Whitaker said. "The club will admit you as Mr. Hardy's guest. You can stand it for one evening. I have come up with a scheme where Hardy can pay me back without humiliation. Not his fault the diamond mine failed. I have the papers my solicitor drew up—you have only to present them to him for his signature."

"Why can't your solicitor present them then?" Herbert asked, a bit petulantly.

"Because it's better coming from a friend in a comfortable place, not in a cold solicitor's office. Hardy has already agreed and will be waiting for you. And, he knows that if I leave this world before he can, the estate will forgive the debt."

A fine motive for murdering a man. Putting that fact together with Miss Townsend's speculation that Mr. Hardy was sweet on Mrs. Whitaker made him a prime candidate.

"I think you are far kinder to him than he deserves," Herbert said, sharing my opinion. "But I will meet with him." He patted his uncle's shoulder. "As long as you promise to eat up Mrs. Holloway's food and get better."

"I'm sure I will." Mr. Whitaker smiled weakly. "Off you go, boy. A sickroom is no place for a robust young man."

Herbert squeezed his uncle's thin shoulder once more then

gave him a good-natured farewell and turned to depart. As he passed me, he swallowed, his eyes red-rimmed and moist.

Was Herbert truly that worried his uncle would die? Or was he simply a fine actor?

I silently dished out soup and added a soft piece of bread to it as the doctor laid a hand on Mr. Whitaker's forehead and felt his pulse.

"And how are we today?" Dr. Burnley asked.

"*We* are three different people in this room," Mr. Whitaker answered. "Mrs. Holloway seems in good health. As do you. *I* am doing poorly. But the custard is helping." He reached for another spoonful.

"It was kind of you to bring up the food," the doctor said to me.

He did not continue the sentiment, but I heard in his tone the wish that I would leave.

"He is to eat all of it," I said sternly as I set out the soup and bread along with a helping of the blancmange. "His lady wife's orders."

Both men softened. "Her will is to be obeyed," Mr. Whitaker said. "Bless her."

"Yes, *Mrs.* Whitaker is likely why you are still alive," the doctor told him.

"I know you think she doesn't deserve me, Burnley, but I assure you, I adore her." Mr. Whitaker took an eager slurp of the soup. "Thank you, Mrs. Holloway. If ever you consider changing houses, please speak to my wife."

Mrs. Provost would not be happy to hear this, but I took it as the compliment he meant. I curtsied politely to both men, thanked Mr. Whitaker for his praise, and left the room.

MR. WHITAKER'S HOUSEHOLD HAD GIVEN ME MUCH TO PONDER. AS I descended with the empty soup tureen and custard dishes, I thought about the way Dr. Burnley and Mr. Whitaker had spoken to each other. Friends who'd known each other a long time, I decided. The doctor's manner, however, was disapproving, as though Mr. Whitaker's illness personally displeased him.

The nephew, likewise, hadn't been what I'd expected. Herbert had exuded fondness for his uncle and concern for his health. He'd inherit the lot, Cynthia had said, but it was true that not every young man relished such responsibility.

I returned to the kitchen and reported that the master had eaten heartily of the custard and was starting on the soup and blancmange.

Mrs. Provost sniffed. "It's nothing *I'd* have given him to eat. We'll see if it settles him, shall we?"

I could not linger to find out. I bade Agnes and Mrs. Provost a good afternoon and departed to walk home.

I let out a long breath once I was out in the street. Carts and carriages rattled past me, streams of horses' breaths fogging in the cold air. The icy winter afternoon, as gloomy as it was, was preferable to the warm hush of the sickroom, where a brave man faced the knowledge that he wasn't long for this world.

Something wet trickled to my cheek, and I wiped it away impatiently. This was no time to become maudlin.

Perhaps my food *would* make Mr. Whitaker better. A person could recover from poisoning if it was caught in time, and he was given good care. Depending on the poison, of course.

I wondered if Daniel could infiltrate the Oriental Club and find out more about Mr. Hardy—particularly whether he'd had opportunity to pour a something foul into Mr. Whitaker's tea or whiskey on Tuesday afternoon. The fact that Mr. Whitaker was still alive was perhaps due to the fact that Mr. Hardy hadn't given him a deadly enough dose but hadn't had the chance to administer another.

I had to push aside my worries for the personable Mr. Whitaker once I reached home, and return to my duties. Tess eagerly asked what had happened, and I gave her a truncated version as we worked.

Today, I started the Christmas pudding, which, after boiling, would rest in the larder for several days before I warmed and served it. Some families enjoyed the tradition of "Stir-Up Sunday," where every member of the family, on the first Sunday in Advent, would come to the kitchen and give the pudding a good stir. Mrs. Bywater didn't hold with such things, she'd told me. Too unsanitary, was her view. I was to start the pudding no earlier than the week before Christmas.

I bade Tess grate the heels of stale bread until we had a heaping bowl of crumbs. She rubbed her arm when she finished, complaining that her elbow would never be the same again.

Into the bowl went thinly sliced orange and lemon peels, raisins, chopped currents, and chilled suet I'd saved for this purpose. Tess cracked open a couple dozen eggs, and I stirred these in with a liberal amount of a good brandy Mr. Davis had chosen for me.

We made enough batter for several puddings—one for Christmas, one for New Year's, and an extra in case any visitors arrived in between. The Christmas one would have the trinkets Mrs. Bywater insisted be stirred into it, though I didn't much like adding inedible things to food. Mrs. Bywater, for reasons unknown to me, didn't worry about sanitariness in this instance.

I had some pretty molds—a domed one and two with serrated edges that would make pleasing shapes. Tess and I spooned the batter into these and covered them with damp, floured cloths, tying them tightly to the sides of the molds. We then set the puddings into pans of water to boil overnight.

Early the next morning, I came downstairs and lifted the puddings from their baths. I set them in the larder, where they'd drain and wait until Monday, when I'd boil one again for Mr. Davis to serve at Christmas dinner.

When I emerged from the larder, pleased that the puddings so far had gone well, Cynthia banged in from the outside stairs, strangely early for her.

She hadn't been to bed, I saw, from her rumpled male attire and disarranged hair. Stayed all night with Bobby and Miss Townsend, I guessed.

Her eyes were wide with distress, her movements agitated.

"Mr. Whitaker has taken a turn for the worse," she announced. "He was very ill in the night, and the family fear he'll not see Christmas."

CHAPTER 6

"This will not do." My voice rang down the passageway, all my ideas of the previous day made topsy-turvy. "This will not do at all."

"But how are we to help him?" Cynthia demanded. "He rallied after your soup and custards, so his nephew said. Bobby and I drove young Herbert to his uncle's house early this morning, after following him to a gambling hall last night, I'm sorry to say. He became highly inebriated, and Bobby and I had to drag him out. We left him staggering into the house on Brook Street but he came running out a moment later, saying his uncle was in a bad way. He was weeping, poor lad. I hurried home to tell you."

I paced the floor, pressing my fist into my palm. What *could* I do? I had no business rushing to the Whitakers' home, no way to prove my theories.

I could send word to Inspector McGregor of Scotland Yard. But he might not be able to look into things until too late, if he took any notice of me at all.

Daniel could stop at the Whitakers' and inquire, as could Cynthia's friends. But Daniel wouldn't be allowed past the kitchen, and none of Cynthia's acquaintances were early risers.

My contemplations were cut short by the sound of hurried footsteps in the passageway. I popped out of the kitchen to see Mr. Davis heading into the housekeeper's parlor. Mrs. Redfern had not yet come down, so I hastened there to see what was the matter.

"Mr. Davis?"

Mr. Davis turned from rummaging in a cabinet where we kept things locked away from the underservants. He held a large black bottle.

"Paul is feeling poorly this morning," he said in annoyance. "Overindulgence, I say. He went to visit his aunt yesterday, and she fed him an early Christmas dinner. He ate heartily and drank just as much. The mistress wants him up and about his duties and has asked me for her favorite bottle so she can dose him. I think he'd be better off with weak tea, but the mistress insists."

I knew what was in the bottle. Mrs. Bywater spooned its contents liberally into servants who complained of the smallest stomachache. It was a very common remedy, and every household I'd worked in supplied it.

"We must go to Mr. Whitaker on the moment." I pulled off my apron and barked a command to Lady Cynthia, who'd followed me. "Hail a hansom, at once."

Instead of upbraiding me for forgetting my place, Cynthia instantly dashed back to the kitchen and out the door, her feet flashing by the high window as she hurtled herself upstairs to the street.

"Mrs. Holloway?" Mr. Davis asked in a baffled tone behind me.

"I will return as soon as I am able," I told Mr. Davis as I hurried to the kitchen. "Tess can see to breakfast. Do not let on I am gone to Mrs. Bywater, please."

Without waiting for his reply, I tossed down my apron and snatched up my coat before following Cynthia up the stairs.

When I reached the top, I turned toward South Audley Street, where the closest hansom stand would be, and found Cynthia already in one rolling toward me. The driver barely halted long enough for me to scramble inside, then we were off at a rapid pace to the Whitaker's home.

Once we reached the house on Brook Street, Cynthia plunged out of the hansom and ran past the portico's elegant columns to pull frantically on the doorbell. I thrust a shilling at the cabbie before I hastened down the stairs and into the kitchen, without bothering to knock.

Mrs. Provost swung from the stove where she was cooking eggs to death, and Agnes's head popped up from where she rolled out dough at the table.

"Mrs. Holloway," Mrs. Provost said, aghast. "What the devil do you mean, bursting in here?"

I ran through the kitchen without explanation, pushing past a startled maid on my way to the stairs. I dashed up them and through the green baize door into the quiet of the main house. On the ground floor, a footman was just opening the front door to Cynthia.

"Quick," I cried to her. "We must stop him."

"Must stop who?" Cynthia stepped around the footman who tried to block her way, and hurried after me as I mounted the stairs to the upper floors.

"Mr. Whitaker," I panted in answer to Cynthia's question.

Mrs. Whitaker herself stepped out of her husband's bedchamber as we reached the second-floor hallway.

"Lady Cynthia?" She took in Cynthia's male attire and then me panting next to her, her eyes widening. Mrs. Whitaker's face was lined, her expression that of one who'd lost hope. "What on earth?"

"Is the doctor here?" I demanded.

"Of course, he is. My husband is very ill, and does not need—"

I charged through the door, bumping past the poor woman in my haste. Cynthia followed me, Mrs. Whitaker watching in bewildered indignation.

"Stop!" I shouted.

Dr. Burnley, who was doing nothing but gazing down at his patient, swung around and gaped at me.

I strode past him and grabbed a large black bottle from Mr. Whitaker's lavishly carved nightstand, a bottle identical to what Mr. Davis had taken from the housekeeper's parlor.

"Have you been giving him this?" I waved the bottle at the doctor.

Dr. Burnley's thin face reddened. "Of course, I have, you impertinent woman. What are you doing in here? Mrs. Whitaker, why has—?"

"It's ipecac." I turned the bottle to show Cynthia its label. I uncorked it and took a sniff, wrinkling my nose at the acrid odor.

Cynthia stared at me. "What is the matter with that, Mrs. H.? Auntie uses ipecac all the time. She swears by it."

"In the diluted form sold by apothecaries, it can be a good emetic, though too much is a bad thing." Mrs. Bywater did like to give sick staff a good hearty dollop. "But if a doctor boils it down to concentrate it, or adds juice from the ipecac plant itself, he can poison his patient slowly, simply by instructing him to take his medicine."

"Oh," Cynthia said, enlightened. "So that when the patient dies, everyone will assume it was from his long illness. They'll even praise the doctor for trying to help."

"You are a *cook,*" Dr. Burnley snapped at me. "How dare you barge in here and disrupt a sickroom? Mr. Whitaker is in a bad way."

Mr. Whitaker's eyes were open, but his lids were heavy, his fingers like sticks where they clutched the blanket.

Dr. Burnley pointed a furious finger at me. "Get out."

I lifted a spoon from the nightstand and trickled syrup from the bottle into it.

"If it is harmless, then take some yourself." I held the spoon out to him. "There's not much here. A tiny amount of ipecac won't hurt you."

The doctor backed away in alarm. Foolish man—the actors in the pantomime had been much better.

Mr. Whitaker's voice rasped from the rumpled bed, while Mrs. Whitaker watched, stupefied. "Burnley? I think you should explain yourself."

Dr. Burnley continued to glare at me. "You have no proof. Neither you nor this … trollop … have any business here." He made a dismissing gesture to Cynthia.

Cynthia did not faint in dismay at his contempt for her. "I'd say the proof was in the bottle, eh, doctor?" she said cheerily. "We'll just take that to Scotland Yard and have it tested, shall we?"

Dr. Burnley lunged for me. I sidestepped him, clutching the bottle to my chest. A little ipecac splashed onto my work dress before I could jam the cork back in.

"Good Lord, Burnley." Mr. Whitaker's voice was faint but stern. "You've just insulted the daughter of an earl who is also the niece of an old friend. Is this kind cook correct? You've been poisoning me all this time?"

Instead of denying it, Dr. Burnley lunged at me again, but Mrs. Whitaker got in his way.

"No." She held out her arms, as though protecting me from an attacking dog. "If you have nothing to fear, Doctor, you will let the medicine be tested. And if you truly have been making my husband and your dear friend ill, tell me why."

Dr. Burnley's jaw hardened. "He has been keeping a mistress." He hissed the word. "He pretends to be so devoted to you, but for the last few years, he has been going to another woman. Betraying you, humiliating you." His eyes took on a new light, a doting one. "I did this for *you*, Angela."

"Not a mistress," I said quickly. This was not a time for secrets —the Whitakers would have to talk through this revelation later. "She is his daughter."

Mr. Whitaker gasped. Burnley had leaned toward Mrs. Whitaker as he spoke and now he snapped upright.

"What are you talking about? This woman is mad." Dr. Burnley glared at Mr. Whitaker while pointing at me.

"It is true," Mr. Whitaker said. "From my misspent youth. Cristina McCafferty is a lovely young lady I am proud to say is mine."

"A by-blow," Dr. Burnley began with a sneer. "My dear Angela, how could he do that to you?"

"I know all about it," Mrs. Whitaker said clearly. "He told me the day he found her. And I will thank you not to address me so familiarly."

Dr. Burnley recoiled as though he'd been slapped. He gazed at Mrs. Whitaker in anguish before he returned his angry glare to me, the woman who'd ruined all his plans.

He charged at me, shoving his beloved Mrs. Whitaker out of his way, ready to beat me to the ground. Cynthia seized his arm, hard enough that he had to waste a moment shaking her off.

I did not want to run and perhaps let him escape, so I looked around for a weapon to take him down. There was a poker at the fireplace, and I raced for it.

Dr. Burnley disentangled himself from Cynthia and came for me. He was nearly upon me when I dodged aside, adept at avoiding a man's fists.

Dr. Burnley hurtled after me, but in the next instant, the large form of Mrs. Provost filled the doorway, a rolling pin raised.

"That will be quite enough of that," Mrs. Provost announced.

I thought she would finish at simply threatening Dr. Burnley, but Mrs. Provost strode into the chamber and slammed the rolling pin into the doctor's middle. The small man let out his breath with an *oof*, and slowly collapsed to the floor, his arm over his stomach in agony.

Mrs. Provost raised the rolling pin again, as though ready to have a go at me, but Mrs. Whitaker once more stepped protectively in front of me.

"Fetch a constable." Her command was firm, and even the formidable Mrs. Provost hesitated. "At once, please."

"I'll go." Cynthia dashed out, light on her feet, and waved imperiously at the maids and footmen who'd gathered in the hall. "You—come with me." She pointed at the footman who'd opened the front door for her. He jumped and complied, the two of them skimming out of sight.

"Mr. Whitaker needs a purge, I'm afraid," I said to his wife. "I believe a dose of morphine is in order as well. From a reputable doctor, mind."

Mr. Whitaker laughed weakly from his bed. "She's a physician and a knight in shining armor as well as an excellent cook. I commend you, Mrs. Holloway."

"Hush." Mrs. Whitaker went to him and leaned down to wrap her arms carefully around him. "Oh, my darling, to think he was taking you away from me."

"I will be well." Mr. Whitaker patted her, reassuring her even though he could barely speak. "Never you worry. I'll sit at the table and eat our Christmas pudding with you. You'll see."

"Humph," Mrs. Provost said. "If I can get one boiled up in time." She switched a glare to me. "I suppose you have a recipe for *that* too, Mrs. Holloway."

CYNTHIA AND THE FOOTMAN RETURNED WITH A CONSTABLE, WHO was skeptical at first, but Cynthia and Mrs. Whitaker convinced him to head for Scotland Yard.

Dr. Burnley was in no condition to run away while we waited. He remained on the floor of Mr. Whitaker's bedroom, clutching his abdomen and moaning.

Inspector McGregor turned up within the hour, Daniel with

him. The inspector was not at all pleased to see me, but he listened to my babbled explanation without interruption, and gave the bottle to his sergeant for testing.

Dr. Burnley, when he could speak again, tried to claim that Mrs. Provost and I had attacked him for no reason. However, with the Whitakers, Lady Cynthia, and the staff who'd witnessed the struggle taking my side, Inspector McGregor brusquely arrested the doctor for attempted murder by poison.

Inspector McGregor betrayed no glee at catching a would-be murderer. He scowled at me as he followed his constables, who had Dr. Burnley in manacles, out of Mr. Whitaker's bedchamber.

"Happy Christmas, Inspector," I couldn't stop myself from saying.

The inspector grunted something, tipped his hat politely to Lady Cynthia and Mrs. Whitaker, and strode from the room.

After I made certain that Mr. Whitaker's servants settled him and his wife, Daniel, who had remained to help, walked us home.

"Thanos has invited James and me to Christmas supper at his flat," Daniel announced as we strolled down Davies Street toward Berkeley Square. "He would be most happy if both of you could join us."

Cynthia flushed, and not from the brisk wind. I imagined Mr. Thanos dithering about sending Cynthia an invitation directly, which would have been most improper. Having it come through Daniel was a wise solution.

"I am spending Christmas with Grace," I reminded them. "But perhaps I could stop on my way home."

"That would be splendid." Daniel smiled at me.

"I will gratefully attend as well," Cynthia said. "After I tear myself away from the very traditional Christmas luncheon Auntie insists on. Both Bobby and Judith are going to their respective families, so I'll have no refuge with them."

She spoke off-handedly but I could see she was quite pleased Mr. Thanos wanted to spend Christmas with her. Perhaps one day, Cynthia would be hosting Christmas feasts with Mr. Thanos at her side.

Daniel threaded his fingers through mine. "The Whitakers will have a happy Christmas after all." He leaned to me. "Well done, Mrs. Holloway."

His whisper wound through me, warming me in the icy December air.

THE NEXT DAY, CHRISTMAS EVE, DANIEL SENT A NOTE TO ME VIA James that a high concentration of ipecac had indeed been found in the bottle I'd taken from Mr. Whitaker's bedside, a much stronger elixir than should have been there. A magistrate, unhappy he had to listen to cases on Christmas Eve, decided there was enough evidence to lock up Dr. Burnley to await a trial.

Another doctor now attended Mr. Whitaker and was giving him the right medicines to help him recover.

I was relieved I'd found the solution in time. The Whitakers were a doting couple, their nephew was a cheerful lad, and now they had a daughter to bring into the family. A happy ending for all of them.

Not, I thought, for the gentleman who owed Mr. Whitaker so much money, but from what I'd heard Mr. Whitaker tell his nephew, he was being kind to Mr. Hardy about the repayment.

I speculated that Dr. Burnley had upped the dose after my visit to Mr. Whitaker, worried that I or Mrs. Provost could help by giving Mr. Whitaker food that would ease his symptoms. Either that or he'd pictured himself comforting the widowed Mrs. Whitaker through the rest of the Christmas season.

Dr. Burnley's arrest also absolved me of Mrs. Bywater's conviction that I'd served a tainted dish at her supper party. Now that I no longer had to worry about the mistress sacking me—for that, anyway—I was free to concentrate on Christmas dinner.

Tess and I prepared the tarts, cakes, and breads on Christmas Eve, and boiled down stock for the soups. Cynthia's father had indeed brought a few game birds to Town with him, which were plucked, cleaned, and in the stockpots before I went to bed.

On Christmas morning, I rose very, very early. The goose went straight into the oven, stuffed at the last minute. Then I had to fix breakfast for the family and servants, followed by cooking the vegetable dishes and accompaniments to the goose, as well as re-boiling the Christmas pudding for a few hours.

Tess and I worked like fury, and just before one, had all in readiness. The soup and fish course went up, the dishes quickly coming back empty. Mr. Davis himself supervised loading the roast goose into the dumbwaiter, then he ran upstairs to receive it in the dining room.

"I'll watch over the rest," Tess said to me as she cranked the dumbwaiter upward. "You go on. It's only Christmas one day a year."

"I hate to leave you to do the rest alone." I was torn, both wanting to be with Grace but wracked with guilt for leaving Tess on Christmas.

"I'm seeing my brother tomorrow for Boxing Day," Tess said. "And Caleb. I'll be all right."

She shooed me away, and I let her. I ran upstairs to change my frock for my best one then hurried out the door before Mrs. Bywater could think of an excuse to need me a few minutes longer.

I hugged Grace hard when I reached Joanna's home and had another happy surprise. Daniel was there, along with James. Joanna had invited them, saying nothing to me.

"I thought you would be with Mr. Thanos all day," I said to Daniel as we went into the dining room, where the table had been decorated with paper chains in lively colors.

Daniel held my chair for me as he answered. "Elgin is engrossed in two problems—one involves calculating the distance to a cluster of stars, and the other is how to concoct a meal to please Lady Cynthia. His landlady is helping with that. I would be in the way."

"Well, I am glad you are here," I said in all sincerity.

Joanna and her cook had put together a splendid meal. There was a fine roasted a hen, a large salad of greens, a dish of stewed carrots, and a heap of tasty, roasted potatoes. Not only that, but Joanna had prepared her own Christmas pudding.

Sam carried it in proudly, bluish flames flickering from the brandy he'd ignited. He set down the domed concoction and lifted the knife, waiting for the fire to die.

"Not a plum in sight," I murmured as Sam sliced into it.

"Pardon?" Joanna blinked at me, but Daniel chuckled.

"I'll have a large helping." I held out my plate when it was my turn to be served, and Sam obliged with a laugh.

We had Christmas crackers—somehow Daniel and I ending up pulling one apart together. I got the larger half, to Daniel's great amusement. We all put on paper crowns and dug into the pudding.

Grace spooned plenty of hard sauce onto hers and eagerly scooped up her first bite. Joanna had made the sauce without brandy, in deference to the five children who'd eat it.

"I have a sixpence," Grace cried, lifting it from her fork.

"So do I," James declared.

"I believe I do as well," Daniel said.

I bit down on something metal and gently spit a coin into my hand. "Sam, really. You don't need to hand out so much money."

Sam grinned. "It's Christmas, Kat. We need a little joy at least once a year."

I knew the Millburns could ill afford passing out sixpences, but Sam had a good heart. I ceased admonishing him and decided I'd somehow slip mine back to Joanna.

It was a wonderful afternoon. I had managed to purchase a charming locket for Grace and one for Jane, a few toys for the younger children, and a secondhand book on mathematics for John, the oldest. His parents hoped they could find a tutor for him so he might continue his education.

The children and Grace exclaimed their thanks, though Joanna now accused *me* of being extravagant.

Joanna had bought me a pretty new notebook with a clasp I could write my kitchen notes in. It was so lovely I knew I'd keep it clean on a shelf rather than use it, but I did not tell her so.

Daniel had also brought various toys and gifts for his hosts and family, nothing too luxurious, but I could tell the items had cost a few coins.

He had nothing for me but sent me a wink as though hinting he'd give me my gift later. As I'd not realized he or James would be here, I'd kept their gifts in the bag I'd brought with me, along with ones for Mr. Thanos and Cynthia.

I hated to leave this happy home, but the afternoon too quickly drew to a close. I embraced my daughter, then Joanna, then my daughter again, reminding her—and myself—that Thursday would come soon.

I left them in that warm, comfortable house, and faced the chill darkness with Daniel and James.

It wasn't long, though, before we were in Mr. Thanos's cozy flat, with Cynthia beaming at us across the table. I wasn't certain I'd be able to digest a second Christmas dinner, but when it was served—roast goose and dressing, with greens and crusty bread—I found that I could indeed eat more.

Instead of another pudding, we had a pear crumble with cream, which was light and delicious.

"Excellent," I declared as I laid down my fork and rubbed my aching belly.

"Auntie raved about your Christmas pudding," Cynthia told me. "Mr. Davis brought it in all aflame. Quite dramatic—he enjoyed it. Auntie said she was pleased you'd made it as she told you, and hadn't it turned out well?"

We all had a laugh about that and explained the joke to Mr. Thanos.

"Truly?" he asked in astonishment. "There are no plums in plum pudding? Then why is it called so?"

"I suppose there were at the beginning," I said, sipping the very good wine Mr. Thanos had poured into all our glasses. "But it came to mean any dried fruit available in the winter."

"How fascinating," Mr. Thanos declared.

He might have asked more about the history of Christmas pudding, but I cut him off by handing out my gifts.

I'd bought Cynthia an inexpensive but pretty cravat pin, which Bobby had advised me she'd like. Cynthia gushed over the brass knot as though it was made of the most lavish gold. For Mr. Thanos, a small case in which to keep his spectacles, which he was always misplacing. For James, a flat woolen cap, much like the ones his father wore, that he donned with a grin.

Cynthia surprised me with a brooch of silver worked in a sinuous pattern, which she told me Miss Townsend, who was an artist, had designed. I pinned it carefully to my dark gown, vowing to wear it only on special occasions, such as this one.

Again, Daniel did not produce a present for me, so I held back the one I'd brought for him. No one questioned us.

After that, I reluctantly declared I must return home, my afternoon out over. Cynthia accompanied me, eager to spend more time with her parents, though she'd never admit that.

Daniel walked us down the stairs, while James remained above to help clear up.

"I will call around later, Kat," he promised as he handed Cynthia and then me into a hansom. "I have many things to tell you."

I did not like how much I looked forward to that.

CHAPTER 7

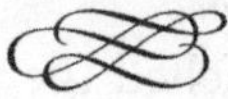

When I entered the kitchen that evening, once more in my work dress, the brooch securely in the bottom drawer of my wardrobe, Mr. Davis came to tell me about the success of the Christmas pudding.

"They ate every morsel," he announced. "Nothing left of the thing, Mrs. Holloway."

"I am pleased the family enjoyed it," I said, deciding to accept the praise and have done. "Though I'm sorry you couldn't feast on the leftovers. There are two more puddings in the larder. Perhaps you can have some at New Year's."

Mr. Davis gave a delicate shudder. "No, thank you, Mrs. Holloway. I won't. Can't abide the stuff."

I hid a smile as he marched away to his butler's pantry. Then I turned to Tess, who was tired but triumphant, and relieved her from her duties the rest of the night.

Once Tess gratefully went up to bed I finished clearing up the mess and started preparations for tomorrow's breakfast. After that, I sat down to write my observations on the Christmas dinner. I noted my appreciation of Mr. Thanos's landlady's pear crumble—I would have to ask her for the recipe.

I did not use the new notebook Joanna had given me for any of this. That was already safely set aside with my cookbooks in the housekeeper's parlor.

As the house grew quiet, and Christmas Day slipped away for another year, Daniel arrived.

"There is no more pudding, I'm afraid," I said as I shut the door while Daniel hung up his coat.

"Ah well." Daniel approached the table, but he did not sit. "In spite of your suspicion that I come here only for your food, this time, I am delivering a gift."

I burned with curiosity about it but pretended not to as I filled the teapot and returned the kettle to the stove. "There is no need for that."

"It is not a matter of obligation." Daniel's smile stirred something inside me.

"Nor for me, but I have one for you anyway." I reached for the bag I'd set safely beside the kitchen dresser and shook out a jacket I'd found at the secondhand shop where I'd purchased James's hat.

Daniel was ever patching the sleeves of coats. This one was of tweed, whole, and well-tailored. A gent must have tired of it and given it to his valet, who'd taken the jacket to the secondhand shop when he'd finished with it.

Daniel's amusement fell away. "Kat, this is a fine gift. Too fine for the likes of a deliveryman."

"It did have a few tears here and there, but I mended them," I said, flushing for some reason. "You can always wear it when you pretend to be a City gent."

"No, indeed. I will treasure it too much to waste it on a disguise. You will see me in it only when I am myself." Daniel's voice went soft. "This was kind of you."

I shrugged, a bit embarrassed. "I'd not have found it at all if I hadn't been looking for something for James."

"I was an afterthought. I see." Daniel's twinkling eyes told me he did not believe that. He set the coat aside and removed a small, paper-wrapped package from his pocket. "For you, my lady. A trifle that I hope you like."

I unwrapped it quickly, not bothering to hide my eagerness. When I saw what lay on the paper I'd torn apart, I stilled, the breath going out of me.

A pretty porcelain frame about two inches by three encased a sketch, done in colored pencils, of Grace. The artist had caught her liveliness, her beautiful smile with its hint of cheekiness, and the brilliant blue of her eyes.

My mouth hung open, and for once, I was speechless. I stared at the picture until it blurred, and a few tears spilled from my eyes.

Daniel was next to me, his warm breath on my cheek. "Presumptuous of me, I know, but I thought it would please you."

He sounded worried that I wouldn't like it. I turned to him, pressing the little sketch to my heart. "Of course, it pleases me. It pleases me to no end." I sniffled and wiped my eyes with the back of my hand. "Who drew this?"

"James. He's quite good at sketching. I asked Grace if she would like to sit for a portrait for you, and she was most happy to. The three of us had the devil of a time keeping it secret."

"Oh, Daniel." My arms went around him while I continued to clutch the picture. "You wonderful, wonderful man."

He knew my heart, did Daniel. Knew it better sometimes than I did myself.

Daniel eased the sketch from me and set it on the table so I would not break the porcelain frame. "And here's me, wishing I'd remembered a sprig of mistletoe."

"We don't need mistletoe, my dear, dear friend."

Daniel's smile made every anxiety I'd experienced about Christmas dinner, Mrs. Bywater and my post, and Mr. Whitaker and family melt away like frost in the spring sunshine.

I pulled him to me and raised my lips to his, showing him without words how much he, and his gift, meant to me.

"Happy Christmas, Mrs. Holloway," Daniel whispered when the kiss eased to an end.

I touched his cheek. "Happy Christmas, Mr. McAdam."

We studied each other a long moment, and then demonstrated once more that mistletoe was in no way needed at all.

THE PRICE OF LEMON CAKE

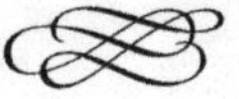

INTRODUCTORY NOTE

When Kat Holloway approaches Lady Bobby Perry and Judith Townsend to help her discover what a young aristo is getting up to in a gentleman's club, Bobby quickly accepts, coaxing a promise of Mrs. Holloway's stupendous lemon cake in return. But the investigation turns into more than a simple spy mission, forcing Judith to confront a painful episode in her past. Both Judith and Bobby must bring their own unique skills to the tricky and dangerous problem.

The Price of Lemon cake is told from Bobby's point of view. Events take place before Book 7, *Speculations in Sin*.

CHAPTER 1

October 1882

"That's a fine one," Bobby Perry said as she lounged in the studio at the top of Miss Judith Townsend's London townhouse. She regarded the painting taking shape under Judith's capable hands with admiration.

Judith added highlights—or whatever it was she was doing—to the golden hair of the lady in the portrait. Said lady was draped across a chaise, lavender skirts billowing, the painted bodice shimmering as the real one would when a beam of sunlight danced upon it.

"I am pleased with it," Judith said in her modest way.

Bobby kicked her legs over her chair's cushioned arm and suppressed her longing for a cheroot. No smoking, not in the studio. Judith's rule. *Too many paint fumes, darling,* Judith had explained the first time Bobby had been ushered into this sanctum. *You'll blow us all up.*

The deprivation was worth it. Bobby would give up tobacco altogether to bask in the dark-haired Judith's aerie.

"Surprised you persuaded good old Cyn to sit still that long."

Bobby sipped the fine brandy Judith always stocked. There were compensations for not being able to smoke.

"A large slice of Mrs. Holloway's lemon cake and a bottle of Beaujolais." Judith's lips quirked into her gentle smile. "It helps that I can make a sketch very quickly."

The subject and their mutual friend, Lady Cynthia Squires, was a restless soul, more at home, like Bobby, in trousers and suit coat than skirts.

"For her family, is it? This portrait?" Bobby waved her glass at the painting.

"Indeed. Something nice to hang in the hall, said her aunt." Judith's brush halted in midair as she tilted her head to decide her next stroke.

"Her aunt means something that won't embarrass them." Cynthia's aunt was horrified that her niece put on men's clothing and went about with Bobby, though she'd already realized she couldn't stop Cynthia doing exactly as she pleased.

"I believe that is the intent." Judith's eyes narrowed as she made a precise dab.

Bobby lifted the brandy to her lips once more, then froze in dismay. "Hang about. You won't let my family bribe you into painting *me* like that, will you? In a frock and all?"

Judith's silvery laughter rang out. "Never, darling. You are much different from Cynthia."

"I don't wish to placate my family, you mean?"

"Cyn is in love with her mathematician," Judith said. "The fact that he might gaze upon this painting of her allowed me to coax her into sitting. Not that either of us admitted such a thing."

"I wish them happy," Bobby said with sincerity. "The pair of them would be good for each other. I hope they produce twenty-seven bouncing babies for Uncle Bobby to spoil rotten. Then I'll hand them back when they need changing and bathing and whatnot."

Judith sent her an assessing glance. "You are fond of children, aren't you?"

Bobby shrugged, trying to hide her embarrassment. She often referred to her brother's children as squalling brats, but in truth they were charming little lads. "They're all right."

"Hmm." Judith returned to the painting, leaving Bobby nonplussed. Judith's *hmms* always held a world of meaning.

"Ever think about having babies yourself?" Bobby asked in curiosity.

Judith hesitated. "I doubt I'll have time for that sort of thing," was her light response. "Too much I want to paint first."

A nice, vague answer. Of course, Judith bearing children required a man to touch her. Said man would likely end up in three pieces at her feet if he tried.

Judith could use an actual sword. Learned it in a foreign land for some reason or other, she'd told Bobby, rather evasively. Judith's life had been far more exciting than Bobby's thus far.

Any further speculation on children or life and its profundity was interrupted by a blast on the speaking tube Judith had installed. No old-fashioned, clanging bells for Miss Townsend's grand Mayfair home.

Judith set her brush on the lip of the easel, lifted the ear horn from its wooden box, and spoke into it. "Yes, Hubbard?"

The muffled tones of Hubbard, Judith's creaky butler, came though the tube, his words too garbled for Bobby to discern from across the room.

"Is she?" Judith asked in delight. "Do please send her up. Or, if she doesn't wish to climb so many stairs, we can come down."

There was a pause, followed by Hubbard's indistinct response.

"Excellent," Judith replied. "We shall await her." She laid the horn back into its box and turned to Bobby, her eyes alight. "It is Mrs. Holloway, come to visit us."

Judith adored Mrs. Holloway, who was the cook for Cynthia's family. Maybe *adored* was the wrong verb—Judith admired and respected her, which was saying a lot. Judith didn't have much use for many people.

Bobby swung her legs down, brightening as well. "What a treat. Do you suppose she's brought any cake?"

"She doesn't exist to bake for us," Judith admonished, then her eyes glowed. "Though what fun if she did."

"Now, there's a thought." Bobby sprang to her feet. "You could hire her away from Cyn's awful relations and set her up here as your cook."

"An intriguing possibility." Judith lifted the brush and touched another stroke to the canvas then wiped the bristles and dropped the brush into a jar filled with oil of turpentine. "But I am afraid I'd be a sore disappointment to her. I eat only simple fare. Mrs. Holloway is far too talented to waste on me."

"I could eat your share." Bobby patted her already ample stomach. "I don't mind."

Judith chuckled, but they could say no more because Hubbard opened the door and stated in his lugubrious tones: "Mrs. Holloway."

He might have been announcing the queen. But instead of the mourning-clad monarch who occupied Britain's throne, a much younger lady entered, one with dark hair, blue eyes, and flushed cheeks. She wore a frock of rich brown that was several years out of date, matched by a modest brown straw hat that sported a few black-dyed feathers.

Her best frock, Bobby knew. Today must be Mrs. Holloway's day out, which meant she was on her way to see her daughter. Nothing would keep her from that, Cynthia had told them, which indicated that what she'd come to say was important.

Hubbard withdrew like a ghost, leaving Mrs. Holloway standing awkwardly in the doorway.

Judith, who'd risen at her entrance, quickly drew a chair forward. "Do sit down, Mrs. Holloway. How lovely to see you."

Mrs. Holloway accepted the chair but perched on it uncomfortably. She was very conscious of her place in life—a highly talented cook in a wealthy household in Mayfair, which put her a cut above most people in service.

However, she held with the nonsense that Judith and Bobby were her "betters." Bobby was in truth Lady Roberta Perry, daughter of an earl. Judith came from a prominent and blue-blooded old family—one half of them practically ran the Foreign Office, the other half, the Home Office. Bobby and Judith might have been born into these privileged households, but Bobby did not see how it made them better than anyone else planted on this earth.

Mrs. Holloway was perhaps a year or two younger than Bobby, but she gazed at them both with the deference of a schoolgirl in the presence of two headmistresses. She planted a dark leather handbag on her lap, enclosing it in her black-gloved hands. The bag was far too small to hold a cake—*bad luck, that,* Bobby mused. Though perhaps she'd left one downstairs.

"I hesitated to approach you," Mrs. Holloway began in her smooth tones. "But I'm at a bit of a loss."

"Not at all." Judith returned to her painting stool and leaned to Mrs. Holloway encouragingly. "We are always happy to help, for dear Cynthia's sake if nothing else."

Bobby hid a snort. Judith might claim they'd assisted Mrs. Holloway in the past in gratitude for her looking after Cyn so well, but Bobby knew better. Judith liked playing detective for the fun of it. She'd had some exploits on the Continent a few years ago that Bobby was just learning about, such as hunting assassins and other exciting adventures. Judith was always up for intrigue.

"Why don't you tell us the problem, Mrs. H?" Bobby paced to the skylight and rubbed a clear spot on the steamy pane. Judith's house lay on Upper Brook Street, and the studio gave a view over the roofs of Park Lane to Hyde Park in the distance.

Mrs. Holloway seemed both reluctant to begin and impatient

to have this errand behind her, but she softened under Judith's kind interest.

"I am looking into a matter for the Countess of Coulson," Mrs. Holloway said. "She approached Lady Cynthia for help—she is worried about her son."

"As she's right to be," Bobby said, turning from the window.

Lady Coulson was the wife of the Earl of Coulson and much despised by Bobby's mother. *A vapid, vacant woman,* Lady Lockwood—Bobby's mother—always snapped. *Lovely to look at but hasn't got the brains of a mouse.*

Bobby's sister-in-law, Eliza, had snidely confided to Bobby that Bobby's mum had once held a grand passion for Lord Coulson. Handsome and athletic, he'd apparently broken many a lady's heart in his day. When Coulson had married the very blonde, very comely chit who'd become Lady Coulson, Bobby's mum had never forgiven her. Still hadn't, though thirty and more years had passed.

Lady Coulson's second son, Terrance, was a wild and untamable rogue of twenty who routinely ran through his allowance and begged for more. His indulgent mother often convinced his father to give it to him.

"I take it you're speaking of the Honorable Terrance Makepeace, black sheep of the family," Bobby said.

"No, the older son, the Honorable William." Mrs. Holloway adjusted her bag minutely on her lap. "Lady Coulson is worried that Terrance has pulled William into trouble, but she is not certain. She fears the wrath of their father, if this is the case."

Bobby stuck her thumbs into her waistcoat pockets. "Coulson might come down hard on her beloved Terrance if he's led William, the heir and apple of his father's eye, astray," she concluded.

"You know the family?" Mrs. Holloway asked her.

"I know *of* them," Bobby said. "Both sons a bit of a loss, in my opinion. Even my insipid brother doesn't like them. Any reason you're keen to aid these rather wet Coulsons?"

"Is that any of our business, Bobby?" Judith asked quickly, probably afraid Mrs. H. would grow incensed at Bobby's impertinence and depart.

Bobby shrugged. "Merely curious."

"Lady Cynthia indicated to me that Mr. William has attended a few of Mr. Thanos's lectures at the Polytechnic," Mrs. Holloway explained in her patient way. "Mr. Thanos believes that Mr. William has great cleverness and much potential, but he is being dragged into the muck by his brother."

"Ah," Bobby said. She leaned back against the windowsill, ignoring the cold of the glass. "Thanos hopes you can save young William—and his brother in the process—in case William proves to be a scientific prodigy. Thanos is too good to his fellow men, if you ask me."

Elgin Thanos, the man Cynthia was mad sweet on, though she'd never say so even if her toenails were pulled out, had an immensely clever brain. He was a bloody genius, able to carry long and complex mathematical equations in his head. He knew a damned sight more about everything than anyone Bobby had ever met. He was also a gentle soul and headlong in love with Cynthia —likewise, torture would never make him admit it.

"In other words, you're not doing this so much for the lofty Lady Coulson, but as a favor for Cyn," Bobby said. "And by extension, Mr. Thanos. Or the other way about."

"Indeed," Mrs. Holloway said primly.

"I commend you," Judith said. "But how can *we* help?"

Mrs. Holloway lost her assurance and looked embarrassed. "Well, it's a bit of a cheek, actually. Daniel—Mr. McAdam—has gone to Ireland, so I cannot ask him."

The blush when she slipped and called McAdam by his first name tickled Bobby. Mrs. Holloway was as gone on him as Cyn was on Thanos. So much romance in the air.

"Ask him what, Mrs. H.?" Bobby prompted when Mrs. Holloway seemed reluctant to continue.

"Mr. Terrance has been taking Mr. William to a gambling club," Mrs. Holloway said. "A rather rough one, on the Strand. Called the Adam since it's near a street by that name. Gentlemen only, of course." Mrs. Holloway's mouth tightened, she clearly having second thoughts about her errand.

Bobby saw Judith realize Mrs. Holloway's intent at the same time she did.

"The penny drops," Bobby declared, her anticipation heightening. "You want me to infiltrate said gentleman's club and see what Terrance and William get up to. And then what? Simply report? Or drag them out by their heels?"

Judith's lovely eyes filled with alarm as she pictured Bobby doing the latter. "Mrs. Holloway, I am not certain that we are the best to ask—" she began.

Bobby cut her off. "Nonsense. Of course, I'll do it. Happy to. Only one thing to ask in return, Mrs. H. If I carry out this mission, will you bring us one of your stupendous lemon cakes?"

CHAPTER 2

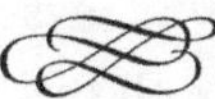

Bobby guessed there'd be a row as soon as Mrs. Holloway thanked them and departed, and she wasn't wrong. When Judith returned to the studio from seeing Mrs. Holloway downstairs, her face held a dark scowl.

"Mrs. Holloway is already remorseful about coming here," Judith began before Bobby could say a word. "She asked me to tell you never mind. She will wait for Mr. McAdam to return and have him assist her."

"Rot that." Bobby flung herself once more onto her favorite chair, a wooden structure with soft cushions designed by William Morris. She retrieved a cheroot from the depths of her pocket, remembered she shouldn't light up, and stuffed it back inside. "Mrs. H. needs a spy, and I'm happy to be one. She did agree to the lemon cake." Bobby rubbed her hands. "I can taste it now."

"Bobby."

Judith's admonishing tone made Bobby's ire rise. "Lord, Judes, you sound like my mother. Only you have to say Rob*er*ta, with your nose turned up so high it's a wonder you can breathe."

"Please be serious." Judith sank to her stool but kept her steady gaze on Bobby. "This idea is highly risky. What if you're caught and arrested? Even if your father could get you off any charge, you'd be humiliated in every newspaper in Britain and beyond. Your father might lock you in his cellar for embarrassing him."

"What should I do instead?" Bobby clenched her tailored cashmere lapels with stiff fingers. "Stuff myself into corset and frock and behave like the insipid society daughter I'm supposed to be? Or wear drab gowns and throw myself into charity work, like the spinster rather long in the tooth that I am? I'm thirty and unmarried—I might as well be dead."

"Do not twist my words, please." Judith folded her arms over her curved waist, her sign that she was uneasy. "I am worried about you. I know you easily blend in with gentlemen in their gaming houses all the time, but this family knows you. Won't Terrance and William be surprised to find Lady Roberta in their midst in a gentleman's suit?"

"Not at all. Their mother and mine made their society debut in the same year. That is the extent of the acquaintance, in the same manner as all titled idiots who went to the same schools know each other. I barely saw Terrance and William growing up, but I heard all about them, mostly from my spiteful mother. They'll have no idea who I am, no fear." And a taste of adventure wouldn't go amiss, Bobby thought, but did not say. Why should Judith have had all the fun?

"But this is a club you've never gone to." Judith rocked a little on her stool, her anger softening to pure anxiousness. "If all titled idiots know each other, as you put it, couldn't someone else recognize you? Friends of your brother's, perhaps? Or one of your childhood acquaintances?"

"My childhood friends either know all about me and wouldn't betray me, or they wouldn't recognize me if I danced naked in front of them," Bobby said with assurance. "You'd be astounded how much people see only what they wish to see. And anyway, I look so much like a bloke, no one has ever tumbled to me no matter where I go. That is why Mrs. Holloway didn't ask Cynthia to run this errand. Cyn can dress in a man's clothes all she likes, but she's very obviously a woman. If she'd cut off her hair, she might fare better, but she refuses."

Bobby rubbed her very short hair, cropped by a barber in the way she liked. So much more comfortable than having all that hair wrapped around her head in styles so complicated it took two lady's maids to dress it. Best thing she ever did was to have the whole mess chopped off.

Judith, whose luxurious hair was a dream to stroke, deepened her frown.

"It is still a risk. What if it's a club where you must have someone vouch for you simply to get inside the door?"

Bobby shrugged. "Then I, like any other disappointed chap, will walk away, hail a cab, and come home. If I don't drown my sorrows at a pub that will let me in its taproom."

"That is another point—what if you get drunk and babble things you should not?"

"Now you are inventing things," Bobby scoffed. "Point the first, I never drink to excess—well, not when I'm trying to be careful. Point the second, what the devil could I babble? I'm unlikely to press my hand to my forehead and say *Alas and alack, I have the body of a woman under all this kit*. And I have no deep dark secrets. I mostly read books, enjoy my cheroots, watch you paint, and get on with my life. The most I'd admit in a drunken fit is that I didn't fancy the latest book by Wilkie Collins." *And that I'm potty about you, dear Judith,* she added to herself.

"It is still too dangerous." Judith crossed her legs, her skirt swinging freely.

Look at her, all tightly wrapped around herself, Bobby mused. She longed to untwist those shapely limbs and end this silly argument with something much more pleasurable.

"I'll be doing nothing more than what I would on a leisurely night out with Cyn," Bobby said. "If you're so worried, come with me."

Bobby only half joked. Judith never had any inclination to dress as a man. She wore frocks designed to her specifications that allowed her less restriction than most ladies' attire and saw no reason to don anything else.

Judith sent Bobby a look that boded no good. "I just might."

She turned her back, took up her brush, and returned to the painting, a signal that the conversation was over.

In spite of Judith's declaration, she was nowhere in sight by the time Bobby was ready to depart that evening.

"She's gone out, your ladyship," Hubbard told Bobby when she inquired.

Hubbard insisted on using the honorific with Bobby and had gone stiff with horror when Bobby suggested he not bother. She didn't press him, however, because Hubbard was a good soul, who put up with Judith's way of life without a word of admonishment or even of judgement.

"Do you know *where* she's gone out?" Bobby asked somewhat impatiently.

"I could not say, your ladyship."

Which meant he might or might not know. Bobby sighed, wrapped a scarf around her neck, and settled her hat. "Never mind. I'll try not to be too late."

Hubbard liked to bolt all the doors at midnight on the evenings Judith didn't have guests. If Bobby didn't make it by then, she'd be sleeping in the garden or trudging home to her old flat on Duchess Street.

She ought to give up that flat, but she didn't want to presume that her newfound understanding with Judith would last forever. Or that they even had an understanding. Bobby was reluctant to broach the subject.

She said her farewells to Hubbard then stepped into Upper

Brook Street, turning toward Grosvenor Square in search of a hansom cab. She soon found one and directed the driver to take her to the Strand.

The Adam Club, which Mrs. Holloway had given them the address of, lay not far beyond Charing Cross railway station. The club was situated in an unprepossessing building of dark brown brick with one small sign on the doorpost to tell passersby what lay within. Bobby alighted from the cab, noting that the club's windows were either shuttered or too grimy to allow her a look inside. The whole place was unnervingly dark.

The hansom rattled away into traffic that was still heavy, even at this hour, the Strand always full of life. Despite the bustle behind her, Bobby suddenly felt very much alone.

She approached the front door as though she had no qualms and rapped upon it.

The portal was opened by the sort of man Bobby expected to see—well-dressed but large and beefy. Portraying respectability but with the obvious strength to throw out any riotous patron.

"Evening," Bobby greeted him cheerfully. "Anyone welcome here? Or do I need to answer the secret questions?"

In some gaming establishments, if one had to ask such things, then one didn't belong there. Bobby had learned to act the rather dim-witted upper-class twit trying to slum, a ruse that worked like a charm. She might not always be admitted to a place, but she wouldn't be bodily tossed to the pavement either.

It also helped that she had a naturally low-timbered voice and didn't have to take on a false baritone. She bounced on her toes and beamed at the bloke while he scowled down at her.

Bobby knew what he saw—a shortish, plump young man who'd grow stout as he aged, with a square face, brown eyes, and clothes tailor-made for him. Probably had money to burn and not enough sense to hang on to it.

The man abruptly stepped aside and gestured for Bobby to enter. Bobby relinquished her coat and hat to a thinner chap who came forward at the snap of the larger man's fingers. The footman, or whoever he was, tucked the coat into the cloakroom and set the hat carefully on a shelf. She wasn't given a ticket—presumably they'd remember whose clobber went with whom.

Bobby gave both men a salute and dove into the bowels of the club.

The door to the gaming room was obvious, as noise boomed from behind it. Bobby pried open the portal and walked into a wall of smoke. Cheroots, cigarillos, and Turkish cigarettes were in every hand or hung from every mouth. The only things absent were pipes, as those would be leisurely enjoyed in a quieter room, not furiously sucked on over games.

Bobby didn't mind the miasma, as she'd have her own cheroot out soon, but Judith wouldn't let Bobby near her reeking like a smokehouse.

The tables were packed with men from the upper and middle classes who thought they had money to spare for this insalubrious hell. No women present, which was interesting. Often seductively dressed ladies, called butterflies, circulated in clubs like this one to distract a man from playing his best.

Possibly no need for that here. These gents were frenziedly throwing money to the tables as though they never needed to eat again.

Bobby found an empty chair and squeezed onto it. If the table's entering stake proved too high, she'd shrug and wriggle back out, but if not, she'd place a bet and blend in.

The game was *vingt-un*. Bobby studied her cards, laid down a few crowns—which seemed to be an acceptable wager—and waited for the dealer to toss her another card. A ridiculous game, she thought darkly as her hand's total passed the required amount, more luck than skill. Bobby's coins disappeared, and she dug into her pocket for more.

As she played, she glanced about for her quarry but did not see them. Annoying waste of time if they didn't turn up. She'd learned, though, from Cynthia's stories of Mrs. Holloway's undertakings, that investigating was often more about patience than exciting breakthroughs.

The night rolled on, Bobby's coin purse grew lighter, and she never saw Lady Coulson's brats. She recognized gents from other clubs and a few friends of her brother, as Judith had feared. However, those lads had never paid much attention to Wilfred Perry's awkward little sister, and they didn't have any idea who she was now.

Bobby was simply a ne'er-do-well the chaps at the clubs had come to accept. There were enough nouveau-riche young men roaming London these days that who was who had become rather blurred. As long as Bobby didn't try to marry anyone's sister, all would be well.

She lingered for hours, playing cards—losing and winning—enjoying a cheroot and some fairly decent brandy, listening to tittle-tattle, and contributing opinions when asked. Gentlemen often derided ladies for nattering on about other people, but in Bobby's opinion, gentlemen could out-gossip ladies any day.

She saw no sign of Terrance or William Makepeace. There were plenty of young men here wagering out of their depth and losing too much, but none were the two sons of Lord and Lady Coulson.

Discouraged, Bobby at last retrieved her coat and hat and stepped into the night, heading for a hansom cab stand.

She reflected as she walked that a great advantage of assuming man's dress was that no one thought a thing about her being on the street alone, even stumbling along to find a hansom.

If she were in skirts, striding by herself in the Strand at half past eleven, she'd be roundly condemned, by those who didn't try to assail her, that is. Even if she'd been out here through no doing of her own—perhaps she'd been abducted and dropped in this street—she'd be ruined and shunned, as though said abduction was all her fault.

In her greatcoat and hat, however, a scarf around her neck against the new-falling rain, no one looked at Bobby twice.

A hansom waited at the closest stand, the cabbie on top half asleep. He came awake as soon as Bobby stepped into the cab and called her direction, and they clopped off.

Bobby made it to the house in Upper Brook Street as the nearby church clocks began to strike twelve.

"Let me in, Hubbard. I'm just in time." Bobby gave the butler a grin as he opened the door he'd been about to bolt.

"Did you have a pleasant evening, your ladyship?"

"Tolerable." Bobby handed over hat, coat, scarf, and gloves as Hubbard reached for them. "But happy to be home."

"Very good, your ladyship. Miss Townsend has already retired."

It was early, by Bobby's standards, but Judith was unpredictable. Some nights she'd stay up until dawn, painting like mad. On other nights, she'd toddle off to bed at eight.

"Then I shall retire myself," Bobby said. "Good night, Hubbard."

"Good night, your ladyship."

Having carefully hung up Bobby's things, Hubbard returned to bolting the doors, and Bobby headed up the stairs.

A light shone under Judith's bedchamber door on the second floor. Bobby took the chance and pushed it open. She had her own bedchamber in this vast house, though most nights she and Judith shared.

Judith was indeed awake, propped up against pillows, reading a book. Nothing unusual in this, but Bobby noted that Judith was slightly out of breath and the book was upside down.

"All's well?" Bobby asked her.

"Oh, there you are, darling." Judith set the book aside and yawned with pretended fatigue. "I wasn't certain whether you'd return tonight."

"Better company here," Bobby said with honesty. "No luck at

the hell. Plenty of gentlemen losing their shirts, but the oiks in question never turned up."

Judith sent her a gentle smile. "Ah, well. Never mind. Are you coming to bed?"

Bobby's heartbeat quickened. Judith in her fine lawn nightgown was a beautiful thing to behold.

Bobby regretfully jerked her thumb at the door. "I should kip down the hall. I reek like a chimney sweep."

Judith beamed her warm smile. "Leave your clothes over there, and all will be well."

Bobby's heart banged even harder. "What an excellent idea."

She disrobed with all speed and soon was burrowing into the comfortable nest Judith had made. Judith turned down the lamp, softening the room with delicious darkness. All as it should be.

Bobby returned to the Adam for three more nights, determined to not let Mrs. Holloway down. She gambled sparingly, making herself walk away from a losing game, and each night she returned home perhaps five guineas poorer than when she'd left.

Judith was always in bed when Bobby returned, ostensibly reading the same book. She never seemed to make any headway with it, marking the same spot every night before she closed it to welcome Bobby home.

Bobby didn't question her. If Judith wanted to pretend she was nonchalantly absorbed in reading whenever Bobby wasn't there, she could do so.

On the fourth night at the Adam, Bobby's vigil was rewarded. Lady Coulson's offspring, William and Terrance Makepeace, swaggered into the Adam Club and eventually joined the card game at Bobby's table.

CHAPTER 3

The Honorable Terrance, in fact, did all the swaggering. His older brother simply looked worried and out of place.

Another man had come in with the brothers and now hovered at Terrance's shoulder as the lads seated themselves at Bobby's table. This gentleman—Bobby gave him the label with reservations—was about double the age of the brothers, wore a well-made suit complete with gold fob-watch, and observed the two with an eagle-like stare.

Bobby had no idea who he was. She recognized nearly half the gents in this place, most of them sons of peers and wealthy nabobs. Many had either gone to school with her brother or now rubbed elbows with him at the grand palaces of White's and Brooks's.

The other half were the up-and-comers who'd made their fortunes in trade and wanted to hobnob with the peers. They might not be admitted to the closed clubs of St. James's, but they could consort with sons of dukes and earls at the Adam Club without restriction.

This man appeared out of place even here. He had a soft face and a full but well-trimmed beard, and his shoulders spoke of much exercise. His eyes, on the other hand, were like steel ball bearings, devoid of any sort of warmth.

He watched Terrance with an intense gaze, though he did nothing to interfere with Terrance's choices of cards or wagers. If the man was helping Terrance cheat—perhaps signaling what others held in their hands—he was damned subtle. Bobby caught no twitch of fingers or brows that might be guiding Terrance, and in fact, Terrance lost a good deal more than he won.

Now that Bobby had located the lads, she wasn't certain what to do. Note all she observed, she supposed, to relate to Mrs. Holloway.

Her focus on the pair was so avid she lost a hand she could have won if she'd been paying attention. As Bobby slid her markers over, she realized she was twenty guineas down. That was her signal to leave the table. Instead, Bobby took a hefty pull on her cheroot and accepted another round of cards.

Not long into that hand, she found the hard-eyed chap's gaze upon her. Maybe she'd been too obviously staring at Terrance and William. Or perhaps he thought he'd found another mark to fleece.

Bobby drained her glass of whisky in a practiced way and let out an expletive when her hand was beaten. The man's contemplation of her sharpened.

Dash it, Bobby was nowhere near as good at this investigation business as Daniel McAdam. He'd know how to discover information without giving himself away.

Bobby held on to her courage and continued playing.

Neither Terrance nor William ever glanced her way, or at anyone else at the table, for that matter. Terrance was fixed on the game, his eyes glittering. William kept his attention on Terrance, except for fearful glances at the hard-eyed man.

William's spying on him too, Bobby realized. *Trying to decide how to save his brother from this chap's influence.*

The game was not going well for either brother. Terrance was playing very deep, and Bobby doubted William could stop Terrance racing to his ruin.

The hard-eyed man gave Bobby another assessing glance, then he removed a folded paper from his coat pocket and handed it to the nearest gentleman at the table.

This gent flicked through the cards inside the paper, grinned, and passed them to the next man in line. Bobby's curiosity grew as the pack moved from hand to hand around the table.

She opened the paper when it reached her, revealing flat pictures in gray monochrome colors. *Ah.* Naughty photographs. Gentlemen often shared such things at the clubs—some of them had whole books of ladies in various stages of undress.

Bobby never minded gazing upon a lovely woman and studied the photographs with interest. Judith was Bobby's only love, of course, but no harm in having a look.

The hard-eyed man had riveted his stare to Bobby while she leafed through the pictures. She felt his gaze skewering her, trying to penetrate her disguise.

Bobby's heart beat faster. She'd told Judith she didn't much worry that she'd be revealed as having the body of a woman, but now she wondered if the blasted man would expose her.

What would these chaps do to her if he did? Bobby had learned some boxing in her day, but nothing that would help her fight her way free of a gang of men and run for home.

She kept her head bent over the pictures, as though examining them thoroughly. One lady was quite pretty, with either blonde or red hair—hard to tell on a photograph that hadn't been tinted. Shapley lass, wearing only knickers, her long legs crossed. She stared with good humor at the photographer, as though having her picture taken without her clothes on was good fun. Bobby smiled back at her.

She felt the man's attention on her lessen, and when she dared look up again, she saw that he'd redirected his scrutiny to William.

Bobby exhaled in relief, then that breath caught. Beneath the picture of the blonde lady, Bobby found a photograph of a comely woman with long, sleek hair and features she knew very well.

She stared, frozen, at the image, her mission forgotten. The woman's dark hair twined about her bare torso. Like the lady in the previous photo, she wore only the bottom half of combinations, her lower legs and elegant feet exposed. The woman peeped at the camera through a lock of her hair, far more seductively than had the blonde.

When the devil had Judith Townsend decided to pose for bawdy photographs?

She looked younger in the picture, so likely years before she'd met Bobby, but still, Bobby thought Judith would have mentioned it by now. She'd always known Judith had lived a colorful life on the Continent, but she hadn't realized how colorful.

Bobby brought the picture closer to her face. Yes, it was Judith's right shoulder peeking at her, and her slim cheek, those eyes that made Bobby melt into a puddle. On her other shoulder …

She peered harder, wishing the lighting in the room was better. Instead of gaslight, the club had candles and kerosene lamps, probably to keep the high-wagering gentlemen from better seeing their cards.

Bobby realized abruptly that the woman in the picture wasn't Judith at all. But a dashed good resemblance. So good, that there was only one thing for it.

She shuffled to the next photograph, barely noting that this young woman was completely nude, her back to the photographer, peering saucily behind her.

Bobby went through the rest of the dozen before she managed to drop the pictures all over the floor.

"Damn," she said loudly, then dove for them.

A waiter hurried to help, and together they picked up the photographs. Bobby palmed the one of Judith's double and slid it into her pocket.

She grinned as she restored the photographs to the paper and slid it to the next man in line. "Bit of flesh always makes me tremble," she said heartily, and the gents on either side of her laughed.

The hard-eyed man would know the photo was missing. But with luck, he might think that it was still stuck under the table or that the waiter had absconded with it.

To her relief, the man seemed to have lost all interest in the photographs. The packet made it to the last player, who laid the pictures aside after he'd had his ogle, but the hard-eyed bloke made no move to retrieve them. Terrance glanced at them longingly, and Bobby saw his hand edge toward them.

Had the hard-eyed man been testing Bobby? Suspecting she was not what she seemed? Unnerving.

She must have passed his little stratagem, because he ignored her for the rest of the game.

Bobby decided this would be her last hand. She threw down her cards and her coins in disgust when she lost and slid from her seat. She moved slowly toward the card room's exit, glancing at other games as though tempted to join them, then shook her head and meandered into the corridor.

As much as she itched to hurry, she knew that running out of the club like the hounds of hell chased her would only draw more notice. She made herself pause in the hallway for several more puffs on her cheroot before depositing the end into a bowl set out for that purpose. Only then did she stride to the foyer, calling for her hat and coat.

It was colder outside tonight. The finer weather of early autumn had deserted London, and chill rain pattered to the cobbles. Bobby adjusted her scarf and resigned herself to trudging down the Strand in search of a cab.

A carriage rumbled to a halt in front of her before she reached

Bedford Street. Bobby recognized the coach and the figure of Dunstan, Judith's coachman, at the reins.

Torn between annoyance and relief, Bobby yanked open the carriage's door and hauled herself inside.

"Following me about, are you?" she demanded as she landed on the seat next to Judith.

The carriage jerked as Dunstan started forward. Even this late, the Strand was full of vehicles conveying patrons to and from theatres, or revelers to soirees and such. The social Season was long over but that didn't stop anyone still in Town from gadding about to every event they could find.

"I am, yes." Judith sat calmly, her shoulder against Bobby's warm and solid. "Concerned for you. And from your present agitation, I had right to be."

Bobby pulled off her hat and tossed it to the opposite seat. Ruffling her short hair, she peered at Judith in sudden realization.

"You've been doing this every night, haven't you? No wonder I find your chest heaving like you've been running and you reading books upside down. You've hurried home and leapt into bed, pretending you've been there all along. Hubbard is your partner in crime, damn the man."

"I'm sorry, darling." Judith sounded contrite but not entirely humble. "I have no wish for you to be harmed because you're excited about helping Mrs. Holloway."

"I don't know how exciting it is." Bobby jammed her arms over her chest, the photograph singeing her pocket. "Interesting, I should say instead. Lady Coulson's sons came in tonight, by the bye. With their evil mentor."

"I saw them," Judith, who'd just accused Bobby of being too excited about the enterprise, came alight with curiosity. "But I couldn't wait for you to come home before I knew what happened. Do tell."

"Not much *to* tell," Bobby said, hoping she didn't dim the enthusiasm in Judith's eyes. "Terrance seems to be heavily under the man's influence, and William is pretending to be. Probably trying to keep the younger lad out of trouble. Don't recognize the bloke playing nanny to them. He looked at me sharpish, probably wondering why I watched them, but thankfully he lost his fascination."

"Oh, dear. Is that why you're upset?"

Bobby reached into her coat pocket and withdrew the photograph. "Chap didn't unnerve me as much as this did. I thought it was you, but then realized it wasn't. You don't have that."

She pointed to a flower just visible on the woman's shoulder. A tattoo, it was called. Sailors collected them up and down their arms, as did men who wanted to prove they were adventurers. Unconventional ladies occasionally had them done as well.

Judith went very still for several moments. Then she reached out her dark leather glove and took the photograph. "Where did you get this?"

"From the chappie with Terrance and William," Bobby said. "He was handing around a stack of lewd photographs, probably to distract the other gents from their cards. There was a lot of losing, that round."

"More to the point, where did *he* get it?" Judith's voice was as steely as the man's eyes had been. "I thought no more of these existed."

Her cheeks burned red in the coach's dim lamplight, and she pressed her lips tightly together.

Bobby regarded her in bewilderment touched with alarm. "If that ain't you, Judes, then who the devil is it?"

"My sister," Judith said. Sudden tears wet her eyes and spilled to her cheeks.

CHAPTER 4

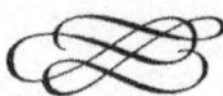

Bobby jerked herself out of her stunned motionlessness and gathered Judith into her arms. Judith rarely cried—almost never. Now she rested her face against Bobby's shoulder, shaking with sobs.

It was difficult not to be flummoxed. Bobby had learned much about Judith's family—their wealth, high standing, and connections to almost every peer in the land on both her mother's and father's side. Bobby's father was an earl, but Judith's parents could buy and sell him several times over, as well as cast him to the four winds ... socially, anyway.

Judith had an older brother, who, like Bobby's, was busy filling his nursery with heirs and spares. All males, of course. Both families had ceased bothering about their eccentric and unmarried daughters, thanks to all the bonny boys springing up.

Nowhere in the narrative had Judith indicated she had a sister, especially one who resembled her so closely.

"What is it, love?" Bobby asked gently. "Did she die?"

Almost every family had lost at least one child, which was a reason the survivors were encouraged to produce as many as they could.

Judith disentangled herself from Bobby's embrace, sat upright, and took a handkerchief from her pocket. Dabbing her eyes, she drew a long breath.

"Forgive me. It gave me a turn, seeing her picture. I thought all those photographs had been destroyed."

Judith still held hard to it, fingers squeezing the card as though she'd never let go.

"It's none of my business," Bobby began. "If you don't want to tell me the tale, that's all right." She was dashed curious, but she knew from experience how painful another's prying could be.

"No, I want you to know." Judith's shoulder bumped Bobby's as the carriage jerked over a hole in the road. "You'd have liked Lucetta. She was a free spirit, determined to choose her own path. Still is, I hope. She is very much alive … I think."

"You *think*?" Bobby's eyes widened. "Good Lord, that sounds dire. What happened?"

"Nothing so awful as you are imagining. Lucetta lives somewhere on the Continent. At least, that was the last I heard from her, ten years ago. She blamed me and cut the tie, but I still worry about her."

"I've changed my mind," Bobby said abruptly. "You must tell me all." She softened. "If I can help …"

Judith shook her head. "It's not an uncommon story." She gave her cheeks a final dab and returned the handkerchief to her pocket, but her eyes remained too bright.

"Lucetta was beautiful and bold." Judith smiled shakily. "Like me, she declared early that she'd never marry a tedious boor and be under his thumb the rest of her life. My parents were incensed with her. They'd already resigned themselves to me being an artist and removing myself from the rules of society. They decided to give up on me, and so expected Lucetta to be the good and obedient daughter. She was to marry a respectable gentleman of the correct lineage and become a model wife and mother. They misjudged her terribly."

"Bit hard on the poor gel," Bobby said with feeling. "I'm no stranger to being pressed to follow that path. Luckily, dear Eliza and Wilfred are so fruitful. Wilfred's children are far more valued than mine would be, in any case." A daughter, in Bobby's family's view, was an appendage, useful only for making a connection with another prominent family.

"As you can imagine, Lucetta rebelled," Judith went on. "She was always more audacious than me. Unfortunately, her adventuresome spirit landed her in the clutches of a bad man. I liked Mr. Arnott—Stephan—at first, and I encouraged my parents to leave her be."

"But?" Bobby reached for Judith's free hand and squeezed it. "There is a *but* lurking in that sentence."

"Arnott was an artist, a photographer. Lucetta met him at one of the parties I took her to. His work was very good, and he was personable enough. I saw no harm in him. He supplemented his income, as many photographers do, by selling racy pictures to publishers, collectors, and anyone else who would hand him the money. I didn't blame him for that—it is difficult to make one's way in the art world, unless one has a wealthy patron."

"Lucetta posed for him?" Bobby asked. "Of her own free will?"

"She was proud to do it. Lucetta said she was helping him. Artists must do what they can to eat, she told me. She was certain that the commission to make him rich would come along any day, and they'd be married."

"But it did not," Bobby supplied.

"No, which turned Stephan bitter and angry. He pressed Lucetta to do more and more pictures, and then he wanted to hire her out to undress in salon gatherings—you know the sort of thing."

Such parties had been all the rage at one time. Unclothed or barely draped young women turned up in the drawing rooms of the rich to pose as Greek statues. Rather silly, in Bobby's opinion, but people thought it showed they were both very modern and had good taste.

"She objected?" Bobby asked.

"Not at first. But Lucetta didn't like having to stand perfectly still, in a draft, while gentlemen walked around her and ogled her. It was one thing to pose for a photograph alone in a studio with Stephan, another to share her body with strangers. She declared she wasn't a courtesan and refused to do any more. But Stephan had already promised her to several more soirees and ribald parties, and he stood to lose a bit of cash." Judith's mouth tightened into a grim line. "He took it out on her."

"The bounder," Bobby growled in rage. "Did you put your boot up his backside?"

"In a manner of speaking." Judith's tone told Bobby she'd not gone easy on Mr. Arnott. "I got Lucetta away from him, and I spoke to friends who made London too hot to hold the man. He fled his creditors to the wilds of Canada, I believe."

"Where there are many bears," Bobby finished with satisfaction.

"I imagine he tried his luck on the gold fields. He was that sort." Judith waved him away. "We've never heard from Stephan Arnott again, which is the best conclusion. I gathered up all the photographs and burned them. Lucetta helped me—she enjoyed it. But our family shut her out." Judith gazed down at the photograph in regret. "They disinherited her, cut her completely. Told me I wasn't allowed to have anything to do with her. Lucetta had ruined herself, and now she must live with the consequences."

"Very compassionate of them. I take it you ignored this command?"

"Of course, I did. I loved Lucetta. I decided I'd travel for a time on the Continent and took Lucetta with me, out of their reach. She deserved a life, happiness. But while she appreciated my assistance in getting her away, she also blamed me for the family shunning her. If I'd not rebelled first—if I'd taken up the mantle of the good daughter and made an advantageous marriage—Lucetta could have had her own life—*my* life—without censure. In her eyes, I stole that from her. Plus, she'd met Stephan through me and my art circles. Her resentment ran deep. I know she simply needed someone on whom to take out her disappointment, but it hurt."

"Poor Judes." Bobby rested her head on Judith's shoulder. "None of it was your fault."

"I knew that, logically, but my heart said otherwise." Judith slid her hand over Bobby's, her leather gloves soft. "It *was* my fault for striding out without a care for what anyone thought of me. I left Lucetta behind to struggle and then founder."

"*Really* not your fault," Bobby repeated. "Lucetta could have cut off the blackguard at any time instead of trusting him, could have asked for your help in leaving home before that."

"I know you are right." Judith's voice was strained. "Yet, I can't help what I feel. One night, Lucetta and I had a terrible row. We were in Paris, living in a hotel. She wanted nothing more to do with me, and I told her she'd be a fool to refuse my help. We said many more things, all of which I regret now. She stormed off." Judith let out a shaking breath. "I've not seen her since."

Bobby saw her pain, which awakened a hurting in her own heart. Judith had kept this locked inside her, trying to put it behind her and move on. But she'd never truly been able to, and no wonder.

"I imagine you didn't leave it at that," Bobby said quietly. "You must have tried to find her."

"Of course, I did. I remained in Paris for a long time, searching, but Lucetta was gone. None of her acquaintance had seen her—or so they said. I began checking the city morgue, just in case. Thankfully, she never turned up there." Judith's grip tightened on Bobby's hand, conveying the fear she'd gone through. "Eventually I accepted that if Lucetta wanted to contact me, she would. About that time, I met Miss Morisot, the artist, and started to paint with her. I was grateful to her for her instruction and decided to stay on in Paris for several years. I never ceased looking for Lucetta, but I also never found her."

"You met McAdam there too." That story Bobby had heard, how Judith had posed as McAdam's wife and flushed out assassins bent on killing men who knew how to make weapons.

Judith's smile returned. "Assisting Mr. McAdam helped take my mind off my worries. I realized when hunting those men that there were far more things at stake in the world than my family troubles."

Bobby disagreed that Judith's worries were of less consequence than the fate of nations, but she kept that thought to herself.

"Is this one of the scoundrel's photographs?" Bobby asked, touching the picture still in Judith's hand. "Or a more recent one?"

"No, this is Stephan's work." Judith's brow puckered. "I swore we destroyed them all. I must discover how this man at the Adam Club got hold of it."

Judith's trembling had subsided, her voice returning to its usual determination. When Judith set her mind on something, woe betide any person, even an assassin, who got in her way.

Bobby's worry eased—Judith upset was not something she liked to see. She preferred that her strong-willed, quietly stubborn lady be free of difficulties.

"Well," Bobby said, trying to sound optimistic. "We'll find out exactly who this chap I saw at the club is, and ask him."

JUDITH'S SOLUTION FOR RUNNING THE HARD-EYED MAN TO GROUND was to interview Lady Coulson's sons.

She arranged to meet them, by methods unknown to Bobby, in Regent's Park the following afternoon. Likely Judith had used the network of servants she seemed to command, starting with

Hubbard and her extremely loyal and discreet lady's maid, Evans.

However the word got passed, at three o'clock, Judith and Bobby descended from the coach and moved sedately to the entrance of the Royal Botanical Gardens in the southern portion of Regent's Park.

At least, Judith strolled sedately—Bobby was bouncing with impatience. She was ready to shake Terrance until he told her all he knew, but she reined herself in and let Judith take the lead.

Terrance and William had actually obeyed Judith's summons. The brothers waited near the gate at the Inner Circle—the lane that bounded the botanical gardens.

William stood ramrod stiff in a fine suit, autumn coat, and tall hat. Terrance, on the other hand, was red-eyed and pasty skinned, with rumpled coat and cravat twisted as though he'd slept in it. From the looks of things, he probably had. William was dressed for an afternoon's ramble in a park, while Terrance still wore last night's evening dress.

Judith halted when she reached them, nodding with extreme politeness. William tipped his hat and gave her a courteous bow.

Terrance belatedly seized his headgear and lifted it the barest inch from his head, but he kept his back rigid. If he tried any sort of bow, he'd likely fall over.

"Bit heavy on the tipple last night, eh?" Bobby asked, letting her voice boom. "Feeling delicate, are we?"

Terrance winced and screwed his eyes shut for a painful moment.

William sent Bobby a startled look. "Hang on, you were at the Adam last night, weren't you? Do I know you?"

Bobby straightened the lapels of her coat, its cut as smart as William's, before she stuck out a gloved hand.

"Robert Perry, at your service."

William clasped Bobby's hand, flinched slightly at her firm grip, and quickly let it drop. Terrance didn't bother offering to shake hands, but then, it probably hurt him to lift his arm. He'd already been well into his cups when he'd arrived last night, and he must have imbibed quite a bit more after Bobby's departure.

"Mr. Perry mentioned that you had a gentleman with you last evening," Judith said in her even tones. "I would like his name and address, please."

Terrance gaped. With his open mouth and red-rimmed, watery eyes, he resembled nothing more than a startled fish. "Why the devil should I tell you that?"

"Terrance." William's admonishment held shock. "Is that any way to speak to a lady? Apologize at once."

Terrance curled his lip. William might be shadowing his brother, trying to keep him out of trouble, but Terrance was by no means docile.

"It's none of her bloody business who he is," Terrance snapped. "Why do you want to know, eh? It's a fair question."

William became more and more distressed at Terrance's language. Judith, who could swear like a sailor when she had a mind to, withstood the onslaught without wavering.

"I have reason to believe he has something that belongs to me," Judith said smoothly. "Or knowledge of it. I will not tell him from whom I obtained his direction, if you do not wish me to."

When Judith began speaking like an instructor at a finishing school, most gentlemen became embarrassed and fell all over themselves trying to be on their best behavior. William certainly flushed and cleared his throat, but Terrance, who must have one hell of a hangover, only glared at her in defiance.

"Blackmailing you, is he?" Terrance chuckled, a sound like a boot on eggshells. "Maybe over some indiscretions with your gentleman friend?" He swept Bobby a knowing sneer that held some admiration. Bobby rolled her eyes.

"Certainly not." Judith's voice became ice cold. William's flush deepened, and even Terrance's sarcasm fled him. "This is of great importance. I am doing you the courtesy of asking you first, before I take up the issue with Lord Coulson."

"You never would." Terrance's aghast answer floated out, his face losing what little color it had.

Bobby, standing a pace or two behind Judith, mouthed, *Oh, yes, she would.*

"It is no matter," William said quickly. He seemed as adamant as his brother to keep his father far from their exploits. "His name is Joseph Moody, and he has a shop where he sells all sorts of things. Moody's Emporium, he calls it. On the Commercial Road, in Shadwell."

Terrance glared at William but realized it was too late to stop him. "A place no lady ought to go," Terrance said with derision. "Have a care for your reputation, love."

Bobby took a step forward. "Have a care for your tongue, lad, or you'll get a punch in the nose."

Terrance looked Bobby up and down. Bobby had no great height, but she was sturdy, and had rather enjoyed her boxing lessons.

"I'm only giving her a friendly warning." Terrance faded next to William, becoming sullen. "Shadwell is a dangerous place."

Judith jotted the name and direction into a small notebook she'd removed from her pocket. "Thank you," she said to William. "Why are you with such a gentleman, in any case? From what Mr. Perry says, he is not the most honorable of men."

"None of your affair," Terrance said, trying to imitate Judith's cool tones, and failing miserably.

"My brother likes to gamble," William said. "I am trying to dissuade him of the habit."

"I see." Judith skewered Terrance with a shrewd gaze. "You owe Mr. Moody some winnings."

"Quite a bit of them," William answered while Terrance spluttered. "Mr. Moody bought up all Terrance's gambling debts from the clubs and now wants to be paid. He follows us about—

Terrance swears he'll win the money he owes, but of course he never does."

"And if he cannot pay?" Judith asked.

"Our father is very wealthy." William reddened again. "Mr. Moody threatens to take the money from *him* if need be. We truly do not want this coming to his attention."

Bobby broke in, "You could always confess all to your dear papa. Let your brother face the music, and be right out of it."

"Obviously, you do not know my father," William said, with the first hint of humor Bobby had seen in him. "We both will bear the brunt. Best we solve this on our own."

"Why are you spilling to them?" Terrance demanded. He focused a bleary gaze on Judith. "Who are you? William only dragged me here because he feared what you'd tell our pa about what we get up to. Friend of our mum's, are you?"

"A friend of Mr. Thanos," Judith said calmly. "He says you have much potential," she added to William.

William started and then looked pleased behind his worry. "Yes, he's a clever gentleman," he said with admiration, while Terrance wrinkled his nose. "I hope to return to his lectures as soon as I can. If there is anything else we can do to assist you, you have but to say the word."

"That will not be necessary." Judith closed the notebook and returned it to her pocket. "Again, I thank you."

"My brother is an ass, but he is right about one thing," William said. "You should not go to Shadwell, not on your own. Perhaps I could …"

He left the offer to escort her there hanging. Terrance let out a taunting snort, then put a hand to his head as though even that effort had pained it.

"Thank you for your concern, Mr. Makepeace," Judith replied. "I never said I would go there myself. Good day, gentlemen."

William tipped his hat, opened his mouth, probably to ask if he could guide her somewhere—anywhere—but then snapped it shut and gave her another polite bow. "Good day," he managed.

Terrance swayed and grabbed William's arm to steady himself. "Tart," he snarled.

Bobby raised one balled fist. Terrance's alarm grew as Bobby came at him, and he hurriedly ducked behind his brother.

William held up wavering hands to halt Bobby's onslaught. "I apologize, Mr. Perry. My brother is an idiot and had a late night. He has no idea what he is saying."

Bobby stopped close enough that the brothers understood the threat was real, though she had no true intention of battling these pups. Scaring them would suffice.

Judith paid the encounter no attention at all. She was already walking along the road toward her waiting carriage, her elegance like a song.

Bobby held out her hand, her gaze on Terrance. "Hand them over, please."

Terrance peered at her from behind William's shoulder. "I don't know what you mean."

"I saw you pinch those photographs from the table last night," Bobby said with conviction. "Thought you'd ogle them at your leisure at home, did you? Let's have them."

Bobby had seen Terrance slide the pictures surreptitiously into his pocket as she'd left the table, and she'd taken a chance he still had them on him. It was obvious he hadn't been home for a good grooming and change of clothes since the club—the stench of him was indication enough.

William, growing more the stern older brother by the moment, turned severely to him. "Give them to him, Terrance."

With a growl deep in his throat, Terrance yanked the folded paper out of his coat pocket and thrust it at Bobby. She glanced inside to see that, indeed, all the photographs were there before she tucked them neatly into her own pocket.

Bobby tipped her hat to both of them. "Behave yourselves,

gentlemen. Oh, just a friendly hint—I'd stay far from Mr. Moody were I you. I have the feeling things are going to become very bad for him. Up to you, of course."

She slapped her hat back to her head and swung away, hurrying to catch up with Judith.

Judith, ahead of her, moved briskly, her skirt swaying with her smart, upright walk. Bobby knew she loved this gifted, clever, and generous woman who could put anyone in their place. Now and always Bobby blessed the day that Cynthia had introduced her to the wonderful Judith.

CHAPTER 5

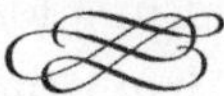

Judith, true to her word, never set foot in the Commercial Road. She sent a flurry of telegrams instead, one to a known associate of Daniel McAdam.

That associate was Mr. Fielding, who on the surface was a respectable vicar, but who'd at one time lived on the other side of the law. Mr. Fielding—or *his* associates—would know how to find Mr. Joseph Moody of Shadwell, and indeed, he did just that.

Two days after their meeting with Terrance and William, Bobby accompanied Judith to a vicarage in the heart of the East End. Mrs. Holloway, informed by Judith that they'd cornered the man causing Lady Coulson so much heartbreak, had insisted on joining them.

Mrs. Holloway carried a box that Bobby suspected held one of her feather-light cakes. Not for them, Bobby surmised, as the box on her lap remained firmly closed and tied with a string during the coach ride across London.

Mrs. H. had changed a bit since Bobby had first met her a few years ago. Instead of trying to hide her shock at Bobby's comfort in men's dress, she now accepted Bobby as she was. Mrs. Holloway was good at that, Bobby reflected. She saw the truth of a person and didn't require that person to change to suit her expectations.

Mrs. Holloway was much more disapproving of Mr. Fielding, who was a wolf in sheep's clothing. He was a slim man, handsome, some ladies would think, with a trim beard and lively blue eyes.

Mr. Fielding met them in the parlor of his vicarage as his long-suffering housekeeper hauled in a loaded tea tray. Bobby sprang up to take the tray, setting it on the tea table in front of Mrs. Holloway. The housekeeper had also brought in the cake, which Mrs. Holloway had handed her upon their arrival, now sliced on a plate.

Mr. Moody was present, sullenly planted on a straight-backed chair. He did not rise when the ladies entered. Mr. Fielding leaned one shoulder against the wall next to Moody, seemingly nonchalant, but Bobby felt Mr. Fielding's tension crackle.

"Is this to be an interrogation by skirts?" Moody shifted his gaze over Mrs. Holloway and Judith, who'd seated herself next to Mrs. H., and let it come to rest on Bobby. "That one *should* be in skirts. Thinks no one knows."

Bobby hid her start. She'd sensed Moody's keen observation at the club but believed he'd dismissed her. Now his assessing gaze held avarice, as though he wondered how much he could blackmail Bobby for.

"Keep a civil tongue." Mr. Fielding's voice was deceptively mild.

Moody flinched, which made Bobby wonder what Mr. Fielding had done to get the man here and make him behave relatively tamely.

Mrs. Holloway, unasked, poured out tea, carefully adding milk and sugar to each cup. Judith handed the cups and pieces of the cake around, as though she served tea at the vicarage every day of her life.

Mr. Fielding took Moody's portion from Judith's hands and

shoved it at the man, which kept Judith from having to go near him.

"Now then, Mr. Moody," Mrs. Holloway began. She was a woman in domestic service, yet she effortlessly commanded the room. "I am thankful to Mr. Fielding for inviting you here, so that I may speak with you. I would like you to cease your acquaintanceship with the Honorable Mr. Terrance and the Honorable Mr. William Makepeace. Forgive Mr. Terrance's debts to you, break the association, and trouble them no more."

Moody's bearded face went slack with surprise, then his lips began to twitch. "Oh, yes? I should do that for you? Why?"

"Because it is the right thing," the unflappable Katherine Holloway returned. "The two young gentlemen do not need you dragging them to their ruin."

Moody's lip twitching became a full-blown smile. "To their ruin? I have that much power, do I? If I drop the lads, what do I get in return? They owe me nearly a thousand pounds. Eh, love? What'll you give me?"

His leer had Bobby coming to her feet. She hadn't actually punched Terrance's nose, but she saw no reason to hold back on this man.

Mr. Fielding swallowed a sip of tea. "A *civil* tongue, I said." The flint in his voice made Moody abruptly lose his smile, and Bobby plopped back into her seat.

"You will have nothing in return," Mrs. Holloway informed Moody. "But turn your attention to other tasks, please."

"Bloody hell." Moody glared up at Mr. Fielding. "You ain't police. I'll do what I choose, and it's no business of this woman with a teapot."

Mr. Fielding emitted a sound like a growl, and Moody snapped his mouth closed.

Realizing Mr. Fielding had things in hand, Bobby slouched back in her chair and had a nibble of the cake. Not Mrs.

Holloway's coveted lemon cake but a lovely buttery one. Bobby took the time to enjoy it.

"You *will* leave them be," Judith stated. "But I have another matter to take up with you. Where did you obtain the photographs?"

Moody blinked at her, clearly baffled by the question. "Photographs?"

Bobby touched the packet of them safely in her pocket. They'd proved to be very interesting and not in the way most people would think.

"The photographs of young ladies you handed around at the club," Judith said. Her back was straight, her dignity splendid. "Where did you get them?"

"Bought them, didn't I?" Moody leaned forward to stare at Judith more intently. "Hang about. One of them was you, wasn't it?" His leer returned.

"Hardly." Judith's crisp tone sent Moody into confusion again. Bobby took another large bite of cake, letting herself be entertained.

"Bought them from whom?" Mrs. Holloway asked.

"A shop, in Paris," Moody said in irritation. "What of it?"

"Which shop?" Judith persisted.

"I don't know, do I? On one of them boulevards somewhere."

"I'll wager you've never been to Paris," Bobby said from the depths of her chair. "You had them from a secondhand shop here in London, whose proprietor told you they came from a studio in Paris. Didn't you?"

"What does it matter?" Moody asked testily.

"It matters very much, indeed." Judith's tone remained neutral, but Bobby sensed her disappointment. "Never mind. I suggest that you release Mr. Makepeace from your clutches, shut down your 'emporium'—I imagine the origins of some of your goods would not stand up to scrutiny?—and try your luck on shores far from here."

Moody sprang up. "Shut your gob, missus. You don't know nothing. I'm finished here."

He swung to the doorway and found Mr. Fielding somehow in front of him. Moody was a few inches taller than Mr. Fielding, but Mr. Fielding was a solid pillar, and it was Moody who shrank back.

"I said, you ain't police," Moody snarled. "Who are you? Your gents only told me you knew something to my advantage. What is it?"

"That it would be to your advantage to not linger in London," Mr. Fielding said without changing expression. "I suggest you cut your losses, leave here, and start anew."

"Start anew? Why the devil should I?"

Judith answered him after she took a calm sip of tea. "Because your shop has already been seized. I know many people who run things, Mr. Moody. As you say, none of us in this room are police, but I have connections to those who instruct the police in their duties. Quite a number of constables are now going over what sort of items you have on your premises. Others will be in wait to escort you to a magistrate, unless you take our advice and flee."

Moody stared at her in stunned disbelief, then switched to Mrs. Holloway and Bobby, as though hoping they'd contradict Judith. "You're lying. You're nothing but a pack of females."

"Packs of females can have extraordinary influence, Mr. Moody," Judith said. "Are we not made to adorn and inspire?" The words held scorn. "I have inspired the Commissioner of Scotland Yard to take a great interest in you and your doings."

Sweat beaded on Moody's forehead. "Damnation. I'll have you for this, the lot of you. I wouldn't sleep soundly, were I you." His hard eyes became even more stony, the look he shot Mrs. Holloway and Judith bordering on brutal.

Bobby set aside her cake with regret, in case she had to help Mr. Fielding throw the man to the pavement. But again, Mr. Fielding placed himself solidly in front of Moody.

"I wouldn't suggest it." Mr. Fielding didn't raise his voice, but Moody studied him uncertainly. "Other gents like the ones who escorted you here are ready to guide you to the river and push you onto a boat. I have men on that boat to make certain you reach another destination. Or a magistrate can send you to Newgate. It is your choice."

Moody glowered. "I don't take orders from trumped-up vicars."

"I'm a bishop now, did you know?" Mr. Fielding informed him. "But it isn't my ecclesiastical associates who are assisting me. It is …" He leaned forward and whispered something into Moody's ear.

Bobby didn't catch what Mr. Fielding said, but it had a profound effect on Moody. He drew a sharp breath, and his face went nearly green.

"You—" Moody regarded Mr. Fielding with stark fear, and then he charged for the door.

This time Mr. Fielding let him go, giving him a wave on the way.

Mrs. Holloway came to her feet. "He ought to be arrested," she said, her disapproval sharp.

Mr. Fielding's lighthearted expression faded as he turned to her. "This is best, Mrs. Holloway. That fellow is a slippery one. If Moody goes to a magistrate, he'll lie like an innocent babe, and the evidence against him will somehow evaporate. He's done it before, which is why he's walking about free to pull young aristos into his power. Much better that he's running for his life to some far corner of the earth."

"If you say so, Mr. Fielding." It was apparent Mrs. Holloway did not agree with him, but she ceased arguing. "I thank you for your assistance. We will take up no more of your time."

"Nonsense." Mr. Fielding's good spirits returned. "Stay and enjoy tea. It isn't every day I have the company of such great ladies."

"Yes, indeed, let us remain," Judith said. "Why let the likes of Mr. Moody ruin our day? This cake is excellent, Mrs. Holloway."

Bobby plopped down and forked up another hunk of cake. Judith was right—it was jolly good stuff.

Judith was not as serene as she appeared, Bobby saw from the stiffness of her fingers as she ate a dainty bite of cake. Judith had hoped Moody would have more information about her sister, and her frustration at his lack was evident.

Bobby kept herself from blurting out her own news, which she'd saved to surprise Judith if Mr. Moody had no further information. She liked Fielding, but the man didn't need to know all about Judith's personal life. What Bobby had to say would keep.

She contented herself with sitting back for now and enjoying the devil out of Mrs. Holloway's butter cake.

AFTER THE TEA WAS DRUNK AND THE CAKE DEVOURED, MR. Fielding saw the three of them to the gate of the churchyard, where he, ever the gentleman, handed Mrs. Holloway and then Judith into her coach. Bobby pulled herself into it after them. She was stuffed and growing sleepy—perhaps she and Judith could nap when they returned home.

Judith thanked Mr. Fielding graciously and he stepped back, waving them off, grinning like the rogue he was.

"Thank you both very much for your help," Mrs. Holloway said as they rolled toward Whitechapel Road. "I will tell Lady Cynthia to inform Lady Coulson that her sons are safe from Mr. Moody's clutches. Perhaps they will have learned their lesson."

From her expression, Mrs. H. didn't believe they would, and Bobby agreed with her. At least Terrance wouldn't learn, but maybe William could keep him tamed after this.

Mrs. Holloway turned to Judith with keen perception. "You

hoped to learn something about the photographs you mentioned. I know it is hardly my business, but if I can help?"

Judith, who would never dismiss an offer of Mrs. Holloway's powers of reasoning, drew a breath to speak, but Bobby cut her off.

"Before you go into the entire, sad tale, I've been doing some sleuthing myself." Bobby pulled out the folded paper that contained the photographs. "Sending telegrams like mad, hither and yon."

Judith's chest rose sharply, and Mrs. Holloway leaned forward, avidly curious. "What are those?" Mrs. H. asked.

"The photographs Terrance stole from Moody," Bobby said.

"One was of my sister," Judith began, morose. "She—"

"Hold on," Bobby interrupted. "I've had a good squint at these photographs. At the backs of them, I mean. Peered hard at them through a glass. The light in here is a bit dim, but perhaps we can see."

She withdrew from her pocket a small mother-of-pearl handled magnifying glass, a surprisingly thoughtful gift from her sister-in-law. She opened the paper, the photos facedown, and trained the glass on the back of the top photograph.

"There's a mark, just there." Bobby pointed her gloved finger at it.

Judith took the glass and the photograph and raised both to her eyes. When Mrs. Holloway, across from her, caught sight of what was on the *front* of the picture, her brows went up, but she said nothing.

"LM," Judith announced after a time. "That's all I can make out."

"I thought it was likely the name of the studio," Bobby said. "One of the pictures also helpfully has the word *Paris* stamped on it. It's quite smudged—these pictures have been passed about a great deal—but I could just discern it."

"I saw nothing on my sister's photograph," Judith said, lowering the glass.

"Because it was not from the same studio," Bobby said. "The one of Lucetta was taken by her blackguard sweetheart in London, about ten years ago, you said. These others are more recent. You can tell from the clarity of the photographs—techniques have improved in the last decade. Also, the backdrops have more modern furnishings in them, and fashions in combinations and corsets have also changed."

Mrs. Holloway nodded, as though approving of Bobby's deductions.

"Ergo," Bobby continued. "These were from a different studio. As I say, I cabled like mad to some chums in Paris, and they hunted down the business for me. The photographer in that Parisian studio informed my chums that she had sold the pictures to a gentleman from London last year—an aristo, not our Mr. Moody. The aristo must have tired of them, or didn't want his wife to see them, so dropped them at a shop that sells such things. Probably got his valet to do it for him." Bobby shrugged. "And Moody found them there, taking them for his own amusement or to confound others with them."

"*She* had sold the pictures." Judith fixed on the pronoun, ignoring the rest of Bobby's speculations. "The photographer is a woman?"

"Yes, indeed." Bobby couldn't suppress her triumph. "She owns the premises and takes portraits—likely dabbles in these off-color ones for the extra income. Calls it *LM Studio de Photographie*. Uses initials to hide her sex because so many want a business to be run by a man."

Judith turned her intense stare on Bobby. Bobby couldn't look away, though she felt Mrs. Holloway's burning interest from across the carriage.

"What does LM stand for?" Judith asked. "Do you know?"

"Lucetta Mercier." Bobby tightened, waiting for Judith's reaction. Would she be excited or unhappy that Bobby had decided to pry? "That's her married name."

Judith stilled, lips parting. "Lucetta—" Her throat worked. "You found her."

Bobby kept her voice gentle. "I appear to have."

Judith continued to stare, round-eyed, then suddenly she launched herself at Bobby, wrapping her in a tight, desperate embrace. Judith's mouth landed on Bobby's face and neck, she exuberant in her shock and joy.

Bobby would love to explore how they could celebrate in this carriage, but dear Mrs. Holloway sat across from them. She'd edged her feet back as Judith's sweeping boots nearly kicked hers.

"A trip to Paris might be wise." Mrs. Holloway's calm tones slid through Judith's mad kisses. "If this lady is your sister, she will want to see you."

Judith unwound herself from Bobby and fished out a handkerchief to wipe the tears from her face. A clean, neatly folded handkerchief, of course.

"She might not welcome me," Judith said.

"Do not be so certain," Mrs. Holloway said. "Am I correct that it has been many years since you've seen her? And that you lost touch?" Trust Mrs. H. to understand the full story from the bits and pieces she'd just heard.

"Yes." Judith swiped at her cheeks again. "It was not an amicable parting. I have often wondered …"

"Go." Mrs. Holloway sent Judith a sage smile. "You must try to make amends. It is clear that you love her still. Now, we have reached Cheapside. If you will have your coachman stop here, I will continue on foot."

She was off to visit her daughter, Bobby understood—the charming little girl who had the same dark hair and pretty eyes as her mother. Mrs. H. couldn't admit she had the daughter, lest she be dismissed from her post, but Bobby and Judith could keep a secret.

"Of course." Judith knocked on the roof and ordered Dunstan to halt. She opened the door for Mrs. Holloway herself, and Bobby leapt out to guide Mrs. H. safely to the ground.

"Do greet your girl for us," Bobby told her. "Here." She fished into her pocket and pulled out a farthing. Any larger sum, and Mrs. H. would be too proud to accept it. "Let her spend that on sweets, or a dolly, or some such."

Mrs. Holloway flushed but took the coin. "Thank you kindly, Lady Roberta." She shook out her skirts on the dusty road. "And thank you both for your assistance. The promised lemon cake will be forthcoming."

"Excellent." Bobby grinned at her. "I await it with lively anticipation."

Mrs. Holloway ducked her head, always humble, then turned from the carriage. Her steps grew eager as she headed for the lane that must hold the house where her daughter lived, looked after by Mrs. H.'s oldest friend.

"I much admire her," Judith said once Bobby was back inside, and Dunstan started the coach again. "A very clear-headed woman. We all should be as steady."

"I agree." Bobby edged next to Judith, hoping for a return to the enthusiastic kissing. "Shall we do as she says and go to Paris?"

"I'd like to," Judith said with faint hope. "But what if Lucetta doesn't want to see me?"

"I wager things have changed. Could be she doesn't believe you want to see *her*. But good for her for becoming a photographer herself. All artists in your family, eh?"

"I'd love to have a look at what sorts of things she's done." Judith's tone turned more optimistic. "Yes, let us plan a journey. Scandalize our families by traveling alone together."

"Hardly alone, with Evans dogging your steps," Bobby said with a laugh. Judith would never leave her lady's maid behind. "We can pretend to be man and wife. Mr. and Mrs. Perry. Such fun." Bobby tried to push aside a qualm. "If you'll have me?"

The smile Judith turned on Bobby transformed the gray London street outside into the brightest paradise.

"Of course, my darling Bobby. Do you even have to ask?"

Bobby's throat tightened. "I do have to ask. You know how fond I am of you, Judes." She drew a breath and then decided to shuck her reticence. "No, not fond. I mean—I love you. There, I said it."

Bobby sat back, her heart banging. Would Judith give her a kind smile and then explain that she didn't share the sentiment? Judith had always seemed just out of reach, like a fine-plumed bird who flew off as one stretched out a hand toward it.

Judith turned in the seat with a rustle of fabric, the scent of tea and buttery cake clinging to her.

"Dearest Bobby." Her voice was soft, taking on the note it did in the dark of night. "The anchor in my swirling world. I love *you*, my silly darling."

Happiness welled in Bobby's chest, displacing the sharp ache that had nestled there. Tears stung her eyes, but she swallowed them down. It would never do to become a blubbering fool.

Bobby hid her shakiness by tossing her already crushed hat to the seat Mrs. H. had vacated. "Well. That's all right, then."

Judith's answering smile nearly undid her. She laid her head on Bobby's shoulder, and they continued home, bumping alone in the carriage together through the middle of teeming London.

ALSO BY JENNIFER ASHLEY

Kat Holloway "Below Stairs" Victorian Mysteries

A Soupçon of Poison

Death Below Stairs

Scandal Above Stairs

Death in Kew Gardens

Murder in the East End

Death at the Crystal Palace

The Secret of Bow Lane

The Price of Lemon Cake (novella)

Mrs. Holloway's Christmas Pudding

(Christmas Novella)

Speculations in Sin

Leonidas the Gladiator Mysteries

(writing as Ashley Gardner)

Blood of a Gladiator

Blood Debts (novella)

A Gladiator's Tale

The Ring that Caesar Wore

Captain Lacey Regency Mystery Series

(writing as Ashley Gardner)

The Hanover Square Affair

A Regimental Murder

The Glass House

The Sudbury School Murders

The Necklace Affair

A Body in Berkeley Square

A Covent Garden Mystery

A Death in Norfolk

A Disappearance in Drury Lane

Murder in Grosvenor Square

The Thames River Murders

The Alexandria Affair

A Mystery at Carlton House

Murder in St. Giles

Death at Brighton Pavilion

The Custom House Murders

Murder in the Eternal City

A Darkness in Seven Dials

Captain Archer Paranormal Historical Mysteries

A Matter of Honor

Mystery Anthologies

Past Crimes

ABOUT THE AUTHOR

New York Times, USA Today, and *Wall Street Journal* bestselling author Jennifer Ashley has more than 100 published novels and novellas in mystery, romance, historical fiction, and urban fantasy under the names Jennifer Ashley, Allyson James, and Ashley Gardner. Jennifer's books have been translated into more than a dozen languages and have earned starred reviews in *Publisher's Weekly* and *Booklist.* When she isn't writing, Jennifer enjoys playing music (guitar, piano, flute), reading, knitting, hiking, cooking, and building dollhouse miniatures.

More about Jennifer's books can be found at

http://www.jenniferashley.com

and

http://www.katholloway.com

To keep up to date on her new releases, join her newsletter here:

http://eepurl.com/47kLL

Made in the USA
Coppell, TX
04 December 2024